To René who always understood everything
and
For Maman Alice

Prologue

Saint-Pierre et Miquelon
February 25, 1912

My very dear Doctor Calmette,

You have told me so many wonderful things about Saint-Pierre et Miquelon that I wanted to share my first impressions of the islands with you before anyone else. My wife Emma and I have been here for a week already.

Since we arrived, it has been snowing every day. When our ship dropped anchor in the harbour, the scene laid out before us was rather sad. Even the French flag flying from one of the many government buildings along the dock could not manage to make the grey setting cheerier or more colourful. That was enough to make our fellow travellers begin to complain about their posting and talk about going home! You had warned me about this kind of cavalier attitude and I am glad you did: My wife and I have decided to avoid their company as much as is possible in such a small colony.

We would much prefer to make the acquaintance of the local population. People here seem very friendly. Yesterday I met people from Dog Island, which I will be visiting once a week to treat patients.

My dear Doctor, I am convinced that the healthful air of Saint-Pierre will be in every way good for me. My medical work should help me become familiar with the pathologies affecting people who live by the sea. You know how interested I am in this field of medicine which our superiors in Paris tend to ignore. And, as you well know, I intend to devote my free time to photography.

Your faithful colleague,
Louis Thomas

One

Settled comfortably in the armchair in the cozy home of his two closest childhood friends, a glass of Scotch on the table next to him, François sighed with contentment. The radiator in the living room purred and spread its warmth generously throughout the room. The doors had been opened to make the company feel welcome. His wool coat, soaked by the spindrift, was hanging above the radiator in the entryway and the woman of the house had placed his gloves and scarf directly on its burning hot cast iron surface. His boots were waiting on the mat right next to it, and would be deliciously warm when he was ready to go out and brave the storm once again.

Now that François had taken off the heavy clothing and accessories of the season, a feeling of wellbeing gradually filled him, caused as much by the warmth of his friends as the comfort of their home.

"Six months this time."

"Yes, much too long," he replied, taking a sip of Scotch.

It had been six months since François had last come to his islands. It was too long, shamefully wrong in his eyes. He had to admit that over the last few years it had become more and more difficult for him to "escape" (that was the best way to describe it, he thought) and come back to Saint-Pierre et Miquelon, where he had grown up.

His career, more successful than he had ever dreamed, took up all his time. Free time for relaxation, hobbies, even just to think, had been surrendered to the compelling need to work harder and harder, to be ever more productive. Certainly, he drew endless amounts of pride from his success. However, as soon as his mind wandered to the islands for even a moment, when he checked his watch and figured out what time it was in Saint-Pierre, pictured his mother going over to the post office—it is eleven o'clock, she is stopping at the corner to share a funny story with a friend—he could smell the tides, the seaweed, the mud from the harbour. It was like a thunderbolt that struck him with the overwhelming urge to go back to the islands, where everything seemed so much simpler, so peaceful, so easy.

He was regularly afflicted by bouts of homesickness. François had never really been able to get used to the thousands of kilometres that separated him from his family, had never really accepted the fact that he could not simply go back on a whim to be among them. For him, there was only one solution: to cross the Atlantic as often as he could. But the irony of life was such that now, when he enjoyed enough success to be able to afford the trip, he had no time to go.

And yet he was sure that as his crossings became less frequent, they also became more vitally necessary to everything that was genuine in him. Somewhere in these foggy islands remained a part of his personality that he had to protect at all costs. He was definitely not an introspective man, but he had an intuitive feeling that unless he jealously guarded his roots, he would lose the fresh perspective that made him successful and prosperous and he would fade into mediocrity.

In Paris, in his architectural firm, no one said—no one would ever dare say—anything about his trips, which usually occurred on the spur of the moment and disturbed many people's plans. His colleagues considered his travels useless and attributed them to a moodiness that was completely foreign to them. After all, what else could he want, now that he had reached the pinnacle of glory in Paris? And, most of all, what could he possibly be looking for on the other side of the world, in this forsaken place where a couple of handfuls of rundown, wooden fishermen's shanties clustered around horrible government buildings?

If his colleagues had bothered to look more closely, they would have realized that this "hole" (as it had been labelled by a colleague who thought François was too far away to hear) was actually the source of his inspiration and creativity.

François stopped the flow of his thoughts and cast an affectionate look on the couple sitting before him. The friendship the three of them shared was one of the riches the islands had bestowed on him and he regularly drew from this well for his inspiration. Their friendship had shown remarkable strength by surviving decades of separations and changes. No matter how long they were apart, the three of them felt as if they had just seen each other the day before whenever they got together, and continued the conversation they had left off as though it was interrupted just a few minutes earlier.

And theirs was a trusting friendship: His friends neither envied his fortune nor the way he hobnobbed with high society when they read his name in the French magazines that arrived on the island several weeks late. Like everyone else, his friends were proud to see him in the glossy photos of *Paris-Match*, but they worried whenever he looked "exhausted" or "his colour was off." "Look, he's even thinner than before!" they sometimes commented, and this health report mattered much more to them than the handshake of some VIP or even a senator.

In return, François was interested in their lives, their work, the current events that affected the island. He followed local politics, took part when he could in activities such as the first day of the deer or rabbit hunting season, and tried to maintain a somewhat thin but strong line between his background and the life he still called "new" after twenty years. These trips back to the islands were his anchor for his successful pursuits in the French capital, which he still refused to consider home.

The three friends had known each other since they were children. They had attended the same school, had the same teachers, and had written their matriculation exams the same year. At that point, their lives took very different paths: His friends had chosen to stay on the island while he decided to go to France. His all-consuming ambition left him no other choice.

In Saint-Pierre et Miquelon, young people have to make a difficult and life-changing decision early in life. Should they stay or should they leave? After graduating from high school, for François and others of his generation, the choice was to stay in Saint-Pierre and work or to continue their studies in France (metropolitan France, they called it), where their youthful dreams might be fulfilled.

Strangely enough it was easier to leave Saint-Pierre et Miquelon for Canada or even the United States. Despite the language barrier, the islanders did not feel so out of place. It was closer, and often they knew a few people there. And they had a lot in common with their neighbours, who lived through the same harsh winters and built the same kind of houses to withstand them, and who also bought snowplows, hockey equipment and big cars, ordering from the Sears, Eaton's, and Montgomery Ward catalogues, which sold everything from face cloths to Permapress sheets to furniture to shoes. In short, the people of Saint-Pierre shared that same daily routine and weather with the rest of the population of the vast continent. In Saint-Pierre et Miquelon the air smelled of iodine and the wind was just as fierce as it was in Newfoundland or Nova Scotia, and the winter clouds forecast the same snow as fell on Montreal or Quebec City.

To go anywhere in North America was like taking the coastal steamer. Many of Saint-Pierre's young people had already visited Canada. They might have gone to Sydney to see the doctor or to Newfoundland for trout fishing or hunting. On the other hand, you could count on one hand the ones who had gone to France; that crossing was a major journey.

François had made his decision long before he finished high school, and there was no turning back. He had always known, even as a child, what he wanted to do for a living: erect buildings. He could remember the exact moment he made his choice. He must have been six years old. Spring had come unusually early that year. Across the road from his house they had torn down an old house and started construction on a new building. The curious boy had followed each step of the process as though it were a magical adventure, with wizards who first produced the foundation and then the rest of the house almost out of thin air, where nothing more than dirt and pebbles had been a few months before.

Every morning, as soon as he heard the workers' hammers, he would jump out of bed and run to the living-room window, where he practically had to be torn away from his post to eat breakfast and go to school. When summer holidays finally arrived, he gave himself entirely to his passion. His widowed mother was relieved by his fascination, which gave her the elbow space she needed to get her multiple chores done.

François was mesmerized by the building site outside the window, glued to the sight of the men installing the shuttering and the slab and the pouring of the concrete, which was a pretext for community festivities during which the strongest men from the area came to help. The grinding noise of the shovels mixing the cement with sand on a square piece of wood designed for this purpose, the sound of water added with a knowledgeable eye, and then the grey mix falling by the shovelful into the frames still echoed in his ears. He remembered the captivating rhythm, slow but robust, a symphony during which each of the workers seemed to play from his own score.

Little by little, he saw the framing take shape, watched as the vertical posts rose up, imagined what the interior walls—"like ours"—would look like as he compared the walls of the living room with the ones being built across the road. He enjoyed guessing where each room would be, how they would be furnished, who would move into the house, where the stairs would go, what the chimney coming up from the cellar to the attic would look like when it was finished, and, at last, he marvelled at the exterior walls and the roof of the house as they were added.

One day, he saw one of the men nail a little evergreen to the rooftop.

"What is that man doing?" he asked his mother.

"When a new house is covered and safe from the bad weather, they nail a little tree above the door. That way, everyone who had a hand in getting the house ready knows he's invited to come over for a drink," replied his mother.

Indeed, one Friday night not long after that, he saw the big bruisers arrive, the same who had helped pour the cement and frame the house. They climbed gingerly up the makeshift ladder up to the front door. For the next few hours he could hear their laughter echoing through the still-empty house. Soon, thought François, the house would be alive with parties, baptisms, First Communions. Magical!

Once the exterior was finished—autumn was nearly here—there was not much else to see. All that was left to do were the shingles on the outside walls and the felts on the roof. These were tedious tasks that required a great deal of precision and fascinated him so much that one evening, when his mother had sent him out to collect some of the broken wood shingles, which had been thrown on the ground for her fire, he had stood stock-still before a partially-finished wall, examining how the shingles were placed one next to the other and nailed at their thinner part to create a uniform surface. For a long time he stared at the last row of shingles, and then, gathering up his courage, ran his fingers along the wood and leaned over to see how they were aligned. He immediately recognized the principle that ensured houses like his own were protected from the elements: rain, wind, and snow. In fact, that day he had the feeling he was reviewing lessons he had learned long ago. This feeling would come back to him often during his long years of study. It was a confirmation—as if he needed one!—that his career had chosen him and not the other way around.

Once the house was finished, he announced that when he grew up, he too would be a builder. No one had anything against that. A carpenter's trade was an honourable profession and paid well. He was given scraps and planks of wood, and for Christmas that year his brothers gave him child-sized tools. From then on, his family got used to seeing him in the basement, sawing and hammering.

At school, several years later, he discovered that, while people in Saint-Pierre et Miquelon built houses in the traditional manner—without plans and following customs passed down from father to son—people in other places had a different way of working. Some of them were responsible for imagining buildings, designing them, producing detailed instructions for every aspect of the construction, and they left the actual work of building to other tradesmen.

That day, almost ten years after he had announced that he would build houses, he refined his plans. He would be an architect. His family was spellbound: an architect? No one had ever seen such a thing in Saint-Pierre. His mother's eyebrows were furrowed with worry: "An architect? That must cost a lot, all those years of school. Where will we find the money?"

A model student, at the top of his class—only spelling and dictations had ever given him cause for concern—he had everything he needed to succeed, as the saying goes. So naturally the high school principal suggested, as he handed him the Governor's Prize and the Parliamentary Award, that François apply for a scholarship to study in France.

Three years later he left the islands with a scholarship in hand, to pursue his dream in France. Many others joined him in exile: a future doctor, banker, lawyer and researcher. Others, like the friends sitting next to him in their living room, stayed behind. Some of them were hoping for a government position, or aspiring to become teachers, fishers, or managers of the family business. Others would soon leave for Saint-Mary's in Halifax or St. Bon's in St. John's, Newfoundland, to learn English before returning to take their place in Saint-Pierre's business community.

At the time, François had bitterly regretted the fact that his friends would not join him in the European adventure. On the dock that morning long ago, standing next to them, he could already feel the distance separating them. He wanted to shout that they were making a mistake, that they were lacking ambition and that a brilliant future was awaiting all three of them in France. However, he had gathered that his friends were happy with their decision, and he felt hurt as he said his goodbyes. In the days and months that followed, his ego let up, and in fact lately he often found himself wondering if his friends hadn't made the better choice.

Their friendship, in any case, had withstood the test of time. Every time he returned he would drop off his bags at his mother's house (she lived alone since his brothers had married), have a cup of tea with her and listen to the latest gossip from Saint-Pierre, and then hurry over to his friends' house. He would sit down in the same chair, his spot, in the living room, and it would feel as if time had stood still.

"The weather is dreadful," his friend said, closing the curtains.

He would have liked to tell her to leave them open, to explain to her that he liked to sit in a comfortable room and watch the wild weather outside, to admire the incomparable spectacle of the winter storm through the sheers, to see the clouds of snowflakes waft up to the yellow lamplight, hear the crunch of snow under the boots of the rare passerby, feel the vibration of the windowpanes shaken by a particularly strong gust of wind—but he did not dare say it.

He could understand his friends' desire to insulate themselves from the elements, to shelter themselves from the unending winter. *It's easy for me to enjoy the storm*, he told himself. *In a few weeks it will be sunny in Paris.* Here, it was entirely different. The months of bitter cold, the unrelenting wind, the blasts of winter that hammered the islands again and again might be pleasant for him, but for the people living on the islands they meant more snow clearing—the back-breaking chore of boring out tunnels through the icy snow to release the doors—and paying exorbitant heating oil and electricity bills. It meant the near-total absence of sunshine, which sent people into the depths of depression. "From this vantage point," as one of his uncles would often say, his request would have seemed surprising and perhaps even insulting.

However, he disliked the heavy curtains pulled across the windows; they blocked the view of the outside from the living room. They reminded him of the iron bars on the windows of Parisian apartments and the wooden shutters in the French countryside, which transformed the neighbourhood or village into a deserted and eerie no man's land. This evening, the drapes were depriving him of the spectacular contrast between the storm outside and the warmth inside the house, of the pleasure of being the jubilant observer who, in his comfortable armchair, knows that only a pane of glass separates him from the biting cold and the deadly gusts of snow.

He remembered, years ago, when he still allowed himself a few moments of carefree time, spending a few days in what his aunt called "the French Heartland." He had had to buy a flashlight to get around in the night in the little unlit village, after the townspeople had disappeared behind their shutters like termites scurrying underground. He had felt very anxious, as though secret horrors and family skeletons were lurking behind the iron bars and wooden ramparts in the manmade darkness. His designs never included shutters or iron curtains and people criticized him for it, but he tried to ignore the criticism and the fact that many clients added them once their house was finished.

"It's like we were in Langlade!" he joked as he tried to make his way through the little village in Bourgogne.

The intense darkness of the landscape, broken only by a tiny beam of light from his flashlight, reminded him of the evening walks on the Langlade beach that he had taken in his youth. He would search for the fox with shiny eyes, a legendary resident of the dunes, according to an attorney of the last century who frightened everyone with his tales of its terrifying apparitions. At least in Langlade the darkness was natural, because there was no electricity. Once past the first uneasy feelings, enhanced by his fear of the horrible beast pouncing up from the night, he would feel embraced by the soft night.

Sometimes, wandering around on his own, François would turn off his flashlight, and in the brief second that it took his eyes to get used to the darkness and locate some distant light (the reflection of Big Louis' kerosene lamp in his kitchen window, for instance), he would feel like he was drowning. Then he would lie down on the fine sand of a tolt, a little knoll near the water. Before him, beyond the waves that murmured their endless laments, he could make out the lighthouse of Île Verte, the dim lights of a sleepy village on the coast of Newfoundland and, as his body slowly attuned itself to the axis of the Earth, he felt as though he had been reborn on the first day of creation.

After a few minutes, he would close his eyes and plunge his fingers into the fine sand—it was cold on the surface but, when he dug a bit deeper, it still held the delicious warmth of the afternoon sun—and, in the astonishing contrast that imprinted the palm of his hand, he felt an attachment to this place that was rooted more deeply in him than anything he could imagine. He had never forgotten these amazingly sensual moments when he wished he could bury himself, like the countless grains of sand around him, deep in the pink dunes and anchor himself to these islands. The day could rise, the sun could shine, he could stay there, or leave, come back in a hundred years or even a thousand, and the warmth captured in these grains of sand would wait for him, at once faithful and indifferent.

It was here that, for the first time, he felt completely in harmony with the Universe—an exhilarating sensation that he hadn't felt since. He did not know exactly when or where his discomfort had first set in: Was it the day he first left his islands, his hands clutching the ship's rail with a combination of fear and excitement? Was it when he attended his first university lecture and he felt out of place in his badly fitting clothes? Or was it when he finally had the chance to work on the most coveted projects, surrounded by colleagues of his own choosing, all highly qualified men but who were lacking in the human qualities that would have been more in tune with his own? In any case, despite his success, the recognition of his peers, and the admiration of those he loved, there was always something missing, a feeling of belonging that he needed to feel whole.

In Paris, he was homesick for his islands, his ocean, his family and friends; he also missed being in close contact with the forces of nature, the wind, the sea. Paradoxically, the architect felt out of place in the middle of the superb Parisian buildings that furnished his everyday life like the set of a play by Marivaux.

Here, on the islands, inspiration came to him in an impertinent gust of wind stronger than the others, in a ray of sun that finally pierced through the stifling fog that had lingered for weeks, in the sound of a crystal clear pond about to be caught in an icy grip. But even so, his inspiration lacked the means to take shape and room to develop.

One day, one of his childhood friends, a highly

skilled surgeon, Professor Emeritus in a Paris medical faculty, set the dilemma out before him: as an orthopaedic surgeon, he too had been forced to go into exile.

"What could I do?" he said, with a wink in his eye. "There aren't enough knees for me in Saint-Pierre!"

"And not enough buildings to build," agreed François, with a laugh.

As he left his friends' house that night, he would experience the pleasure of walking in the bad weather, and just as he had felt on the dune, he would find himself both overcome by the force of nature and sheltered by its whirlwind. All the way down the road he would see the reassuring lights in kitchen windows, guiding the pedestrians through the winter nights, and have no fear of losing his way. Walking past certain houses, he would peek in at fathers, mothers, and children, going back and forth from table to kitchen sink, and imagine the smell of the food cooking, the cheerful sounds of conversation and laughter as they ate supper together. One of the mysterious customs on the island was that heavy curtains were never hung from kitchen windows, only in the living room. François could watch life going on in houses he had known all his life, those that had withstood the seasons for over a century as well as the new ones built on the foundations of the old. As an architect, for him these were the moments when a house became a home. In a well-designed home, the heat from the kitchen reached into the smallest nooks and crannies, the light banishing any worrisome darkness, the sounds of daily life giving every room a reassuring sense of being lived in. In bad weather, every wallboard and window sash seemed to enclose the inhabitants like a cocoon. Every house he designed, François tried to recreate the comfort and wellbeing of his childhood, using tricks and techniques to convey the warmth of his home where, even after his father had died and despite the weight of his absence, he had never been afraid.

But my goodness, how he loved storms! To be honest, the bad weather was the reason he visited the islands in the winter. The fury of the unleashed elements was invigorating, filled him with energy, shook him out of the drizzly, depressing, and dingy atmosphere of Paris. Here, he felt alive, even if he were never anything more than a minuscule grain of sand in the unchanging order of the world. The unique blend of snow and sea salt on his lips as he walked around the Saint-Pierre waterfront in the middle of February was a nectar he often dreamed of as he strode up and down the streets of Paris, pulling up his scarf to avoid the smell of exhaust pipes.

When he had visited them, the time before last, while they were sitting around the dining-room table and talking again about the miserable winters they had experienced, he had tried to explain that he enjoyed the bad weather and the feeling of being at the mercy of the elements. No one had taken him seriously; well, almost no one. His friends' daughter, Émilie, had flashed a brief smile in his direction, a delicate gaze that suggested she knew exactly what he meant and that like him, she deplored the fact that others did not understand what that euphoric sensation was like—a feeling that, on this tiny island which was nothing more than a deck of a ship moored in the middle of the vast Atlantic, they had permanently escaped a shipwreck.

Where is she tonight? he wondered, exasperated.

He could have asked the question out loud, but his friends would have no doubt found it strange. In any case, they would not necessarily have been able to answer him. At her age—*sixteen, maybe*, he thought, without certainty—Émilie would no doubt be able to come and go as she pleased, without letting her parents know where she was. As long as she was back at seven o'clock in the evening, everything was fine. She might be at a friend's, or at the skating rink, looking for the handsome young skater or the hockey champion who might take her by the hand and skate around the rink once or twice. *In my day, we didn't have a skating rink*, he thought, smiling to himself at the memory of hockey games on frozen ponds, the frequent falls caused by a blade getting stuck in a tiny wave that had suddenly become a bump of ice.

He took a sip of Scotch, listening with one ear as his friend told him about the last time he went deer hunting in Langlade, and half-heartedly following his stories about trips down the Belle-Rivière and the Des Mâts brook. Curiously, in order for these Tartarin's tales to enthrall him, Émilie would have had to be there, sitting in the little red armchair, her lively eyes catching his. Sometimes, during the conversation, she would have seemed to smile in his direction, watching for his reactions as though she knew in advance what he was thinking and what he was going to say. He missed their silent exchanges, and the story which, ordinarily, would have entertained him and incited a great deal of banter, seemed to fall flat. Something special connected him to Émilie. In her presence, the solitude that often seemed to imprison him dissipated a little. In her intelligent and honest gaze, a little mischievous at times, he felt understood.

The idea that he might have to leave tonight without seeing her made him fidget a bit in his chair. Then, a little embarrassed at not paying attention to his friend's story, he forced himself to pick up the narrative: the deer had just fallen, he was about to describe the way the carcass of the animal had been quartered alongside the bushes.

The three of them heard the door of the entryway open, squeak on its hinges, then the sound of boots being tapped on the threshold to get the snow off them, and lastly the front door being opened and then closed forcefully, the way children are told to do so they will not "heat the sidewalk" in the winter. François could just barely keep himself from breathing an eloquent sigh of relief.

Émilie quickly took off her winter jacket and boots, looking up the hall with vivid interest to see whose coats and accessories were spread out on the radiator. She paused for a moment to admire the handsome silk Paisley scarf, lined with cashmere—he obviously had expensive taste—and the kid gloves in the shape of his hands. She could feel his presence, in these simple objects, an intimate connection, and took a moment to catch her breath as she looked at them.

He's here!

An hour ago she was at the skating rink, spinning around on the ice with her friends, looking out of the corner of her eye at the good-looking hockey player skating with his friends and occasionally breaking suddenly in a cloud of ice to impress the girls. For Émilie, it was not the skater that impressed her as much as the skates, "real ones." Try as she might to stop with the energy and precision the boys displayed, her blades did not allow her to do the same. Girls had to be satisfied with white figure skates with toe picks, jagged teeth on the end that, according to what was written on the box, made it possible to perform *artistic* steps.

When she asked for hockey skates like her brother's, her parents had given her a funny look. She decided it was best not to mention that she also dreamed of playing hockey. *Here we go again*, she sighed. *I don't see things like everyone else.* She often thought this, but never dared to say it out loud.

She wrote it down though. She wrote profusely and secretly. Neither her closest friends, nor her brother, nor her grandmother, nor her parents had any idea that she spent hours writing in her diary. Putting everything that happened to her down on paper, all the contradictory emotions that troubled her, gave her a way of working things out or getting over them. Once she had explored whatever was on her mind by writing it in her diary, she was filled with a peaceful contentment that calmed and comforted her whenever she reread the pages, even in her worst moments of insomnia and anguish.

She had so much to say in these notebooks that she filled one every year. The more she wrote, the more she realized she had strange tastes; she imagined most of her friends felt the same way about her. Often, too often perhaps, she experienced emotions that seemed the opposite of what she should be feeling. For instance, the funnier the situation and the more people around her were laughing, the sadder and closer to tears she became. In those moments, a crushing weight would suddenly fall on her shoulders, for no apparent reason, and she would feel as if she carried the pain of all humanity. Usually no one noticed, and in a few minutes she could compose herself and face life again. Every time she emerged from this struggle between her reason and the unfathomable distress that sapped her vital resources, she felt a little older.

Often, she felt as though she lived a double life. One was visible and ordinary, the other parallel, identical on the outside but a completely different experience from the first. In her other life, she seemed to watch herself evolve and observe the people and events around her as though they were in a film or a novel. The only way she had found to describe this odd separation from herself was to compare it to when photos, because the subject had moved while the photograph was being taken, appeared blurry and superimposed—as though the photographer had taken the soul by surprise.

Maybe, she sometimes said to herself, *I haven't been developed properly.*

Writing was her daily refuge. She tucked every element of her life into her diary, her reaction to books she read, descriptions of people she met, her doubts, fears and wishes. The process itself of writing things down was a physical sensation, a sensual pleasure, a comfort. She always used the same type of notebooks (Clairefontaine brand, spiral) with French-style graph paper pages that were just glossy enough to make her think her Waterman fountain pen was skating around the rink. She always used the same pen, and always put the little pink blotter, stained by blue ink marks, on the last page. She could not bring herself to replace the blotter, as though she were afraid her words would disappear along with it.

Taught by a Latin teacher who believed that form mattered as much as content, Émilie drew a margin down the left-hand side of the page and wrote the date and a title inside the margin. It was a comforting, child-like habit typical of a careful and studious young woman.

She spent long hours with her notebook, wrapped in a blanket of utter happiness. Everything was possible in writing, and everything was allowed. Her prolific reading had made that abundantly clear.

Outside of this secret garden, Émilie played all the games other girls her age enjoyed: She hoped boys would look at her and find her pretty, she tirelessly leafed through catalogues in search of the latest fashion that would make her irresistible; but then, in a split second, for no reason at all, everything would come tumbling down and she would be standing back watching herself, as though her soul had momentarily vacated her body. She would feel ridiculous and have an irrepressible urge to cry, cry enough tears to drown. In these moments, all that remained were the comfort of pen and paper.

Today, everything was fine. Late in the afternoon, as she was having a cup of hot chocolate with her best friend at the skating rink, her friend said, "Uncle François is here."

"I know," Émilie replied laconically.

What else could she have said? The emotion she felt from the minute he set foot on the island would be incomprehensible to her friend and everyone else she knew. She was sure of it. No one would understand even if she tried to explain.

"He was at grandmother's for tea this afternoon, and then he's going to your place."

She thought at first that the lights around the rink were turned off, as they did when it was about to close.

But no, that was not it. This place—her favourite place that welcomed her every Thursday and every weekend—had suddenly lost its lustre as soon as she knew that François was headed over to her house. There was only one thing she wanted to do: go straight home. Forget the snow!

Émilie took a deep breath and went into the living room. He was facing her. With the elegance she was so drawn to, François stood up to greet her the way he always did, as if she were a grown woman instead of a sixteen-year-old girl. She looked deep into his dark eyes as she approached him, and could see that he was relieved. So he had been waiting for her! He had been worried she might not come home. He opened his arms and hugged her, giving the customary kisses, one on each cheek, and she sat down in the little red armchair across from him.

In that magic moment of their reunion, she felt as though she had crossed over to her other existence, the one she had eloquently christened "my extraordinary life" in her diary. Her blood flowed more quickly in her veins, she sat up straighter, she felt clever, mature, like a grown woman…whole.

The contact between Émilie and François was so subtle and smooth that no one around them noticed how intense it was. For François, however, Émilie's affection was as palpable as if she was blind and touched his face to recognize him at each visit. Her unbounded admiration, this inexhaustible and undemanding affection she showed him, set off equally strong emotions that reminded him of the feelings he had on the sand in Langlade, a deep serenity and a heartfelt belief that he was finally where he was meant to be. Émilie's gaze, at once demure and penetrating, was nothing at all like the blind adoration of a schoolgirl infatuated with an older man, someone she could dream of without fearing that he would become bolder. When he looked in Émilie's eyes, he saw, instead, that she accepted him unconditionally, without having to suffer from this eternal schism between his past and his present. He also had the sense that he had something to give her as well. He was not sure what, but it was certainly something she had never asked of anyone else.

Completely overwhelmed by the intensity of that moment, Émilie allowed herself to become lulled by the conversation which had quickly resumed. She wanted to observe, to listen to him talk, all things that she would carefully write down in her diary later, even if it meant staying up part of the night to do so. In a few days, when he would be leaving, she would have this detailed account of his visit that would help her fill her days until he returned, a little pebble beach between two banks of fleeting happiness. For the moment, it seemed to her that she was only completely alive when he was near her. After a minute or two, François turned to her and she happily joined in the conversation.

The day after the snowstorm, day broke under a magnificent sun. The wind continued to howl. Émilie was awoken a little earlier than usual by gusts of wind coming in from the open sea and rattling the windowpane. Her whole room seemed to shake. She decided she may as well get up.

Émilie did not really like the fine weather, those

postcard days when every wave, every cloud and every ray of sunshine was so neat and tidy. But today, she was eager to go out and watch the sea rise in anger and, it seemed to her, carry off her overflowing emotions.

She especially enjoyed it when the storm ended, when the worst was over and nature thought it was finally time to calm down. She felt that she wouldn't be disappointed this morning: Although she couldn't see the ocean from her window, the moans and creaks of the window pane let her know the direction and the force of the wind. Since most people found her taste in weather unusual, to say the least, she knew she would not have a lot of company on the shore.

On the islands, people took note, almost religiously, of fair-weather days on their calendars and agendas. Those incomparable days when all the elements—from the wind to the sun, from the landscape to the seascape—joined together to create of the islands a true paradise. It was so rare that they wanted to write down all the details: what they did to celebrate the occasion, whether they had a picnic and where or with whom, and especially what the "high temperature" of the day was, proudly announced on the radio by the weather service thrilled to be able, for once, to be the bearer of good news.

"It's odd," her grandmother had remarked as she wrapped her scarf around her face and put on her woollen mittens, "you don't like going out for a walk unless the weather is terrible."

Émilie did not answer; she had wondered the same thing herself and tried numerous times, unsuccessfully, to come up with a reasonable explanation.

Bundled up warmly to face the blustery wind from the sea, Émilie headed for the wharf and then, courageously, for Pointe aux Canons. The ocean greeted her with a slap of cold wind that took her breath away. Doing her best to catch it again, she walked out to the shore, where she could be as close as possible to the rolling waves.

It was too bad, she thought, that in Saint-Pierre, unless you walk for a good hour out to the coves at Alumette or Savoyard, it was hard to get close to the ocean. A wharf, a breakwater, or in this case the port itself got in the way of getting close to the giant. It was not like Langlade; there, on stormy days, you could climb on the dunes and be at one with the ocean, stand within reach of its waves, feel its angry spray and foam on your face.

She finally reached the spot she was looking for, between the Île aux Marins and the cliffs of the Route du Cap. From here, she could see the monster, far behind Petit St-Pierreits, waves lead-coloured despite the sun, their foamy crests, broken off of the waves by the squalls, floating over them like an eerie mist. In the distance, the windswept coast of Newfoundland, flecked by large ice patches, emerged in a rare brightness. There was not a boat in sight; no one would have been foolish enough to take to the sea.

Despite the cold, Émilie took deep breaths, filling her lungs with the odours of iodine, seaweed, and even the pungent garbage from the port. Without thinking, she tasted the damp, salty air that always reminded her of the blocks of butter she was sent to get at the Olivier farm every summer, and that the farmer's wife carefully wrapped in waxed paper.

A particularly strong squall nearly knocked her to the ground as she made her way along the slippery stones and she resigned herself to walking back up the hill to the road, which was sheltered from the windy salt-shore. It was here that she caught sight of François, walking along the other side of the road. Camera in hand, he was examining some old buildings that were from another age, a time when fishing, tall ships, rope-makers, and caulkers still gave life to the island, the golden age of the "terre-neuvas."

Nowadays in the port of Saint-Pierre, people spoke Gallician and Basque, and the Spanish trawlers that ploughed through the waters near the Grand Banks, two by two, had replaced the sailing ships from Saint-Malo and Granville. The warehouses filled with salt cod in the early years of the colony and then with crates of alcohol during the Prohibition in the 1930s now languished in a slow and anguishing decline, their siding, roof shingles, and window frames lifted off by one gust of wind after the other.

Émilie walked over to François, overjoyed at their chance meeting. For once, there was no one around, no appearances to keep up, no faking interest in a boring conversation. As she was crossing the street, he turned in her direction and waved vigorously at her. He hoisted the strap of his camera back up on his shoulder and watched her move towards him.

Émilie glowed with happiness; she was almost running in her eagerness to get to him. *When was the last time someone looked at me like that?* François wondered, touched by her spontaneity.

Heaven knows why, but women were interested in him! He was never without women to go out with, companions who would spend an evening with him, a few weeks, occasionally a few months. His social standing, his success, his very comfortable income—François was modest, he would never think of calling it "wealth"—made it easy to meet people this way. He often thought it was more a question of a woman's pride in "catching" a successful architect, the thrill of the conquest, than it was about being interested in him. This doubt made him hesitate to talk to them about anything serious; he had never tried to describe his childhood or his career or his deepest desires, even to the most intelligent of the women he met.

"What are you doing out here in this wind?" François exclaimed when she was beside him.

"The same thing as you are, I imagine," laughed Émilie. She gave him a kiss on each cheek, her lips icy and salty at the same time.

He started to laugh: Only she could talk to him unpretentiously like that. He had noticed that people did not speak to him the same way anymore. In the last few years, they seemed to talk with him differently. Was it out of respect or embarrassment? Did his fame and fortune intimidate them? Some, indeed, seemed impressed, and he suspected that even people who disagreed with him completely treated him with kid gloves. But not Émilie! With her, it was quite the opposite. When they were at a family dinner, or having a relaxed conversation with friends as they were the night before, nothing he said escaped her. She commented on it, argued with it, made it a point to stand up to him every time, as a point of honour, as though she were chatting with a schoolmate.

Sometimes François noticed that his friends looked a bit nervous, no doubt worried that their daughter was going too far. *They don't understand either*, he realized, saddened to see a limit to the vast expanses of their friendship. On the other hand, he liked everything about Émilie. Nothing she said shocked him; the fears he could sense under her friendly teasing and chiding, her sensitive attention to people and things, and even her thoughts that seemed so close to his.

She took his arm as though they were used to walking together. They strolled along the shore, then turned left on a little road that led up from the beach. François stopped in front of an old house with a tambour, a removable porch that protected the inside door from the weather. Snow had piled up during the night and the driveway had not been cleared, a sure sign that the house was abandoned. Against the inside wall of the tambour were some empty flower pots that must have once held the magnificent red and pink geraniums that traditionally brighten dull days and grey seasons.

Peering at the lace curtains pulled shut, she could imagine the kitchen table next to the stove, the chairs carefully lined up, the framed image of the Virgin Mother right next to the schedule of the tides and the barometer. She could feel the penetrating, paralyzing cold of the room where there used to be a blazing fire...life suspended. She shivered. He looked at her a moment, as if her thoughts had led him, along with her, into the abandoned kitchen. Then he grabbed his camera and began to take pictures.

"What's so special about it?" she asked.

As far as she was concerned, there were dozens of houses just like this in town and this one was far from being the most beautiful.

"Look at the tambour. It could be a simple square

box. But it isn't; instead, there's that nice trim up at the top. Look carefully. In a few years there will be no more houses like this."

She did as he asked, listening attentively until he finished talking. She looked at the snow hugging the stairs up to the entryway, untouched by footprints, forming a splendid arch between the steps and glistening in the sunlight as pure as the first day on earth. This is what the islands must have looked like before the settlers arrived, she suddenly realized. These few metres of virgin snow were a miniature of that unspoiled universe.

When he had finished taking pictures, François took her arm and led her down another street. On this Saturday morning, the day after a big storm, the place was deserted. Émilie had the dizzying sensation of being free from the laws of time and space. They walked, without any set destination, through this winter decor where the everyday landmarks had been erased by the snow and wind, where there were no cars in the lane or passersby in the streets; there was only the raw glare of sunlight—so rare at this time of year—and of course, especially François, holding her arm, their breath mingling in the white whirlwind blown by the harsh and persistent wind. The whole scene transformed their walk into an escape from reality. *Perhaps I've slipped into that other life of mine, the one that is invisible,* she thought. And with that, Émilie who usually chose to analyze every little detail, let herself focus fully on the present moment and rely on her memory for the rest.

A few minutes later, François stopped in front of another house, its shingles—worn down by mist, rain, and snow—had lost all colour. This time he walked right up to the house and began to take pictures.

"You can't tell me it's pretty," she said, a little put off by all the attention he was paying to something she did not find attractive.

"Come here," he said, as if he had noticed her doubts. "Look at the way the unpainted wood is warped. And there, where the snow is sticking to it...Doesn't that remind you of something? No? Don't they look like the waves the wind carves into the sand on the dunes? And look at all the shades of grey, of white. See how different they are? This is so beautiful."

So he, too, had been struck by the magic of the untouched snow, but instead of seeing eternity in it, the way she did, he had thought of the sand on the dune. *Well, she thought, I guess he is more down to earth than I am!*

In an effort to please him, she tried to see the town through his eyes. As they went from house to house, she studied the shingles greyed by the seasons and the houses leaning into the winds like the stubby evergreens on the cliffs of Langlade, the marks of a past she had, up until that point, paid no attention to.

He was fascinated by the low, boxy houses built in the last century, bourgeois residences or simple fishers' homes which had always seemed to her so old-fashioned compared to the North American style houses all the rage among young couples these days.

Exasperated, he declared, "All of this is going to disappear now that people are buying prefab houses. How horrible! You may as well order meccano from the Eaton's catalogue. You see, these houses here were built to last. If you look carefully, in the simplest fisherman's shanty you will see some detail, a little frieze, a decoration that has the sole purpose of making the house more beautiful, of showing how proud they were to build it."

"The way you are, when you're working."

"Yes, the way I am."

It was just like her to get right to the point. He was passionate about his work. From the time he was a child, admiring his own house, he had never tired of the textures of the materials, the angles, the balance that you had to bring to the whole project. Actually, it was a miracle that happened every time a building was completed, however big or small. He especially loved looking at the blueprints when it was all done, seeing it through new eyes and discovering a new bit of himself in it, an extension of his personality, a *je-ne-sais-quoi* that made the building his and his alone.

"The carpenter who took the time to make these little patterns in the doorway—and I'm sure he had lots of other things to do—but he did that so that, year after year, whenever people look at the house, they would know it was him who built it. I use details like that in my designs too," François explained to her. "Depending on the location, I'll use different kinds of wood. You know, some of them change when they are weathered, so that after a few years the whole building looks different. I'm known for using wood with concrete and glass. In some places, wood isn't used to insulate walls the way it is here. But wherever I use it, it adds something unique and local to my buildings."

Émilie drank in his words. If he had been in his architect's office in Paris, his colleagues would have listened distractedly as he spoke. Here, where people bought prefabricated houses and formica was replacing hardwood furniture, he would have been met with polite smiles and patient explanations about how quickly a prefabricated house could be put up, the "clean and practical" quality of these new materials that could be washed with soap and water and did not have to be dusted day after day.

"Of course," he added, "I take pictures of all these houses to give me ideas, but also because they are a dying art. I want to honour all those workers who showed me the way. What is left here, today, is nothing compared to what we had in the past..."

She listened, hanging on his arm and his words, nodding from time to time but not saying a word. She was busy rearranging the way she saw the world around her. She stopped suddenly, right in the middle of the street, and turned towards him. He saw her face light up with such a bright and meaningful expression that he sometimes wondered whether she really needed to speak for him to understand her.

"Since you're talking about buildings from the past, I have something to show you if you'd like. They're old photos that have just been found in an abandoned warehouse. I saw some of them in the studio, and apparently there are hundreds of them."

"Photos? Where did they come from?"

"From a man who is said to have lived here at the turn of the century. A doctor, apparently. Wait...what's his name? Doctor...Thomas, that's it."

"Well, let's go!" he exclaimed like a little boy. He grabbed her hand and led her, nearly running, to the town square in front of the church, where the photography studio was located.

Their laughter rang out, sweet and clear, above the church bells chiming the half-hour. It could be heard in every corner of the town square.

The unrelenting winter wind followed them through the door into the little shop. The room was divided into two parts by a long counter that also served as a showcase, where photo albums bursting at the seams were crowded together under the plexiglass window. At the back of the room, a heavy, black velvet curtain hung in a doorway, hiding the actual studio. The store was mostly frequented by customers looking for passport photos, which were essential because the residents of Saint-Pierre et Miquelon had to go through Canada to get anywhere they might be going. The photographer was also busy with portraits of children posing piously for their First Communion; it was a local custom to give out these photos with boxes of sugared almonds or sweet rolls to family and friends.

"Just a minute! I'm coming."

A muffled voice came from the back room. The photographer was working.

The two of them walked up to the counter, took off their gloves, tuques, and scarves. Émilie pointed to some of the photos, laid out on black velvet.

"Look!" she cried, obviously enthralled.

She was pointing to a picture of the shore they had just left. In the foreground, capelin were drying over hundreds of fish flakes oriented towards the sun; in the background stood big houses, most of them gone now. The mountain, as the hill behind the town was called, just as bare centuries ago as it was now, cut off their view from what was behind.

François leaned over. He was drawn to something different, a grand residence that reminded him vaguely of things he had seen in his childhood, and outbuildings including a big warehouse where piles of salt cod and dried capelin were stored.

"That's the old Folquet building," announced Jacques, the photographer, as he stepped out of his studio to see a young customer to the door. This young man was evidently a bit agitated at the sight of this important person who built houses all around the world, and who had been the subject of conversation in his home for several days now.

"Around 1914, I'd say."

François straightened up and shook his hand. The two men knew each other quite well, since they were about the same age. They had not gone to the same school though; one had gone to the Catholic school, and the other a public school that a priest (or was it a nun?) had once baptized "the Devil's School." Jacques had salt-and-pepper hair and a pleasant, honest face. He was tall and slim and was wearing brown corduroy pants and a sweater with suede elbow patches that made him look like a perpetual student. He turned to greet Émilie, whom he knew well, having taken her photo at First Communion and again at Confirmation, and more recently for her passport.

"Do you want to see the others? Hold on."

He motioned for them to follow him behind the counter and into a corner of the studio where boxes were stacked. He opened them haphazardly and pulled out an assortment of glass plates, prints, and enlargements that he spread over his work desk.

"There are so many of them, I haven't been able to develop them all yet! And the problem, François, is that there is no note, no indication...I have to tell you, dating them and finding their locations is quite a puzzle!"

"But Jacques, where in the world did you find them all?"

"Oh, that's quite a story! A few months ago, a friend and I went to an old warehouse where the Prohibition building was, you know, the one near the Boulot bridge? My uncle had just sold it and asked me to clear it out. Under a staircase, I found two old crates that contained glass plates, all neatly placed in straw to protect them."

"So they've been there a long time, eh?"

"For sure! And it's a good thing I was the one who found them, because you know where they would have ended up..."

He certainly did know! François had never been able to understand why people loved their city dump so much that they threw out all kinds of treasures. They said they were dirty, tarnished, rusted or, worst of all, "germy." As if they could catch scabies or old age from these things!

So old ladies who, for decades, had jealously guarded their belongings, would decide overnight to throw them in the dump: wooden kitchen tables tossed out and replaced by formica, and oak headboards replaced by wrought iron beds, claimed to be "so much easier to look after." The same fad of modernity pushed homeowners to tear down their old houses and buy prefabricated ones in Halifax. François could easily imagine what fate these photographic treasures would have met had they fallen into the wrong hands.

From the pile of photos displayed on the counter emerged a forgotten view of the island at the turn of the century, with its buildings and houses, ships, docks and especially its people, men who worked on the open sea, women and children, public servants, Terre-Neuvas and Newfoundlanders. Fishing dories, capelin and cod drying on the shore, winter and summer scenes of the Langlade dune or the gully in Miquelon, religious ceremonies—communion processions, celebrations for the mariners—all the details that offered an engrossing portrait of life on the islands by an artist who had a heart-felt wish to see and understand everything, but also to explain everything, in black and white and without a word.

"I was trying to figure out who might have taken these photos, until old Léon remembered that a Doctor Thomas used to be seen around here, taking pictures with an odd-looking camera. Léon could even recognize him in some of the photos. Hold on," he said, shuffling through the piles scattered around him, "I'll show you what he looked like."

"Here he is!" he announced proudly, holding an amazingly sharp photo under their noses.

The photograph had been taken on Dog Island. It was a view from the high-water mark looking out in the direction of Tréhouart Cove. A wharf, some houses, and the salt-works could be seen, and farther back, neigh-bourhoods on the island that had long since disappeared. Two men dressed completely in black were standing on an ice floe just off the bank; the contrast between the men and the dazzling white snow was startling. From the bank, a third person was watching the scene.

"The fellow in front, the one with the beret, is definitely the fisherman who owns the dory. The second one, right in front in the fur coat, that's Doctor Thomas."

"Can you pass me the magnifying glass?" asked François.

Jacques passed him the magnifying glass that he always kept nearby, and Francois took a close look at the photograph.

His feet straight forward, his eyes staring out to the open sea, his body stiff, his hands at his side, the doctor's stance and style were a strong contrast to the more relaxed appearance of the two other men, who were standing with their hands in their pockets, watching rather indifferently, as though they had seen all this before. On the other hand, the doctor seemed flabbergasted by the sight of ice floating on the water.

François felt oddly touched by the emotion emanating from the snapshot, and he lowered the magnifying glass.

"Have a look," he told Émilie, passing her the lens and photo.

Now it was her turn to delve into the past. As usual, she commented aloud on her discoveries. "You can see a white collar, a stiff one, under his coat. You can tell he isn't from around here. He is so well-dressed! And a fur coat! My goodness, to look at him, you'd think he was about to jump in the water," she added, moved by the photo without understanding why.

"What do we know about that doctor, Jacques?" asked François.

"Not a whole lot, unfortunately. We know he came here in 1912, that he was posted in Miquelon—you should see the photos of Miquelon! Gorgeous! One day he went back to France and we never heard any more about him. I don't know why he would leave all this behind. It's pretty mysterious..."

François and Émilie looked at each other. Outside, the siren was beginning to screech, announcing it was noon. The store would close and the entire town would sit down to eat. Jacques saw them to the door, eager to go home like the others and spread a serviette over his lap, pour a nice glass of red wine, and dig into the steak and french fries his wife had promised him that morning. An hour and a half later he would be back at the studio. If he wanted to take a nap, there was no time to lose. Closing the blinds in the window, he called out: "If you want, come back this afternoon! I can set you up in the back, where you'll be more comfortable to look at all the photos."

People were already hurrying home. A few cars were headed up from the wharf. Standing still on the sidewalk, François and Émilie stood out from the crowd of people milling about, as though they had just arrived in a time machine and had not yet adjusted to the new world around them. Should they, too, learn to comply with the habits of Saint-Pierre? Without a word, she looked at him. Émilie, who was usually so frank and daring, could not manage to find the words. She wanted to invite him to come back with her in the afternoon, to continue looking at the photos.

"I can't," he replied, before she could even open her mouth. "I promised my aunt I'd visit, and she's expecting me."

Émilie put on a brave smile, as though she had not foolishly been hoping that he would accept her invitation. Still, a few hours stolen from her daily routine would have been so precious.

"Maybe another time," she murmured.

Without a word, François leaned towards her and kissed her on both cheeks, held her close for a moment. Émilie placed her head on his shoulder; there was a silent tenderness during this brief moment they shared. Then, regretfully and without a word, they turned and walked off in separate directions.

The leaden shroud that had lifted from the city this winter morning and drifted off to sea suddenly fell over them once again, threatening to suffocate them both.

Two

"Jacques, I need a favour…Jacques, can you hear me?"

Communications between France and Saint-Pierre et Miquelon left a lot to be desired and put a man like François, who was not known for his patience at the best of times, on edge.

"Jacques," he continued, leaning even closer to the machine, as though he hoped to get closer to his listener.

Never did he feel the distance that separated him from his loved ones as cruelly as he did when he telephoned them. The delays in transmission made it easier for each person to wait his turn, the way René Olivier did at his telegraph in Langlade: "Need fresh bread for Monday delivery, over to you." "Message received, will tell Jeanne, over to you." Or the way the captains of the trawlers did it: "On our way to Saint-Pierre, over." "Need the pilot tomorrow six o'clock, over." Between the nearly inaudible voices and static electricity (as they called any noise they could not immediately identify), François felt the full extent of the distance—an abyss.

That morning, he was persistent. After hanging up, he took a deep breath and dialed the number again.

"Jacques?"

This time the connection was good. The photographer in Saint-Pierre and the architect in Paris could hear each other clearly. How long would they be able to talk?

"I would like to buy a selection of Doctor Thomas' photos. You know, the ones I saw in your studio a few months back. I want large prints, mounted and ready to hang in my office. Can you do it?"

The desire to have the photos had hit him suddenly, after he had been thinking of the piles of black and white photos on the counter of the studio, and especially of the picture of Dog Island. No doubt, the memory of the delicious morning spent with Émilie was part of it too.

As soon as he had returned to Paris, François had had his own photos processed, the ones he had taken on the shore that morning. He thought they had a particular texture, probably because at the moment he was taking them Émilie's presence by his side had influenced his point of view, or perhaps being momentarily released from his solitude had transformed his vision.

The image of the mysterious doctor standing on the shoreline ("ready to jump in," as Émilie had said) rarely left his mind. He was intrigued: Why would a physician, undoubtedly very busy, have decided to become an ethnographer? Why would he have so tirelessly observed, in minute detail, a way of life that was foreign to him and in which his colleagues surely had no interest whatsoever?

"Photos? Of course," replied the photographer, enchanted with the order, "but which ones? How many? There are hundreds, and I haven't even finished developing all of them yet."

"Let Émilie choose them for me. As many as she wants. I have room."

By entrusting her with this responsibility, François hoped to make up for the missed opportunity to spend some time together that afternoon and regain some of the cozy intimacy that had enveloped them for an instant before evaporating into the misty noon air. But he had another reason: He had an intuition that her choices would be perfect, the ones he would have made if he had the time to do it. She would go directly to the essential photos, uncover the most beautiful and the most likely to move him. By giving her this role, he was confirming the precious connection that bound them together and that, he felt, she still had doubts about. He hoped to erase the infinite sorrow he had seen come over her for a second, before she regained her courage.

Through these photos, chosen according to her own tastes and priorities, and which he would hang all around his office, Émilie would become a permanent part of his everyday life in Paris. When exhaustion would overtake him and he would fall asleep on the big leather sofa across from his desk, instead of going home to an empty apartment, she would be there—along with the islands—two inseparable parts of a whole.

On the other side of the world, at the end of the telephone line, Jacques did not seem to find anything strange in François' request. During their short visit to his studio, he had felt the harmony of their connection, a very discreet emotion that had not escaped his experienced photographer's eye.

The two men talked a little about the order and how it should be shipped to France before turning to the weather ("in Saint-Pierre you could cut through the fog with a knife, the last couple of days," "blazing sun in France") and then on to trout fishing.

"Good, then, I'll look after it. I'll talk to her about it," Jacques said. He had to hang up because a customer had come into the studio.

François hung up the receiver, satisfied as always at having taken care of something. He was above all a man of action. Gifted with an enormous capacity for hard work and a contagious energy, he considered every matter with equal part enthusiasm and rigorous attention. "Everything is a series of steps," he often explained. "The greater the challenge, the more stages there are to pass through, that's all. Intelligence consists of pushing the process as far along as possible."

Preoccupied for several weeks with his discovery of the doctor, François had decided to do something about it. The first thing to do was to surround himself with the work of the enigmatic Doctor Thomas. A photographer himself, he was in a good position to appreciate the doctor's technique, his explorations, and especially the patience required to produce such a collection of photos. The spontaneous shots, combined with the rich composition and the quality of the details, spoke volumes about his artistic talent, especially since the camera he would have used at the time was not nearly as sophisticated as the ones available today. François was determined to track down Doctor Thomas. *He can't have fallen off the edge of the earth*, he reminded himself time and time again, *especially if he left all this behind*.

He would have to arm himself with patience. Since

he did not like the waiting any more than the absence, and since he was forced to put up with both, he got back to work with his typical single-minded dedication. He was used to cutting himself off from the world to create and to work, and now satisfied to have taken the first step towards solving the mystery of Doctor Thomas, he put all thoughts of the island out of his mind and returned to his role of well-known architect whose work so pleased his Parisian clientele.

A few days later, when Émilie was on her way to buy bread as she did almost every day, the photographer called her over from his doorstep.

"Come in for a minute, would you?"

He recounted his overseas conversation with François. Jacques did not add any of his own comments, which suited Émilie, "as if he found it perfectly normal that I would be asked to do this." The request nearly knocked her off her feet, but she made sure no one could tell. It was a priceless gift, a special gesture. "The photos are for him," explained Jacques, "for his office."

So François was giving her the chance to shape his environment, to put her own mark on his daily life! By asking her to do this favour, he was proving that she had a special place in his life. She could not get over it, and filled page after page in her diary in her desire to dissect its meaning.

Doctor Thomas was now part of her life, as were her family, friends, teachers, and François. As soon as she found a free moment—the skating rink was closed for the season, so that made it easier—she would go to the photographer's studio and methodically review the photos Jacques was continuing to develop whenever he had time. He had set up a little spot for Émilie to work behind the velvet curtains.

Protected from curious stares, she was starting to sort out her choices. She could never stay long (an hour at a time, if that), but every time she felt as though she were watching a history of the islands unfold before her eyes—rewinding, at high speed, an uncut version—because the doctor, as she called him, seemed to have made a documentary of every aspect of island life.

More than anything else, she wanted to know more about his own life. Was he married? Did he have children? Why did he leave? Where did he go? What kind of medicine did he practice? Did he spend a lot of time caring for his patients or did he prefer to rush through his work so he could travel all over the countryside, through the snow, on the ocean, or around the docks? The sheer number of photographs was an indication that he spent a good deal of time outside the hospital.

During a supper conversation, Émilie had mentioned to her family that she was interested in Doctor Thomas' photos. She simply explained that she was helping the photographer sort and catalogue the prints. It was not because she was concerned with appearances or worried about indiscreet assumptions that she did not reveal her affection for François; it was simply because she had not found a way to put it into words, and sensed that others would have no idea what he meant to her and be tempted to discount it as a young woman's crush on an older man. Only Jacques shared her adventure, out of necessity but also because, since their first visit to his studio that freezing January morning, he had shown himself to be worthy of her trust.

Émilie's parents were not in the least surprised by her new project. It was fascinating, and besides, Jacques' studio was right next door, so it was very convenient.

"You should go to the library to find information about Doctor Thomas," her grandmother suggested. Like everyone else, she had heard about the doctor but had no idea what had become of him when he left the island. In the *Journal officiel*, there might be a bit of information, or at least some mention of his comings and goings.

She had followed her grandmother's advice, taking the dark stairs four at a time to the library. The room had large windows overlooking the port. On each side, in huge glass bookcases, the bound volumes of *La Vigie* and *Le Réveil*, two newspapers from the islands that dated back to the 19th century, were carefully arranged, as were the volumes of the *Journal officiel*. Despite a careful search, she could find no trace of the doctor. It was as if he had passed through the islands without leaving any trace other than his superb photos that captured every detail of daily life: ice cutting at the Frecker pond, capelin drying on the shore, washerwomen in the stream at L'Anse à Miquelon, shipwrecks, First Communion and Corpus Christi processions, burials. The man had gone everywhere—hunting, fishing in dories to catch squid, on sleigh rides in the winter, with seals on the sandbanks by the Goulet.

"When did he find time to look after his patients?" she commented one day to Jacques, who was having enough trouble trying to finish the inventory of the glass plates.

Choosing the photos for François was not an easy job. Émilie approached the task like a school assignment, dividing it into several steps. First she examined all the prints, one by one. Then she discarded the ones which were simply teaching tools, like the one that showed a motor being installed in a dory in dry dock ("a Lashtrop," Jacques said; "I remember my grandfather bought his in 1913") and the ones that showed public events that may have been important at the time but which did not hold much interest now (a shipwreck against the Savoyard cliff or a war ship in the harbour).

She spent a long time on a series of photographs taken at the hospital. One of them showed an operating room; you could clearly see the inert patient on the table and a group of doctors and nurses who seemed to be marvelling at the surgeon's dexterity. It revealed quite a bit about the period, but this scene did not seem entirely appropriate for an architect's office.

In the soft light of the little room, she put down the photographs for a moment and began to think about the old hospital where Doctor Thomas must have worked, and that had been converted into a "hospice," as nursing homes were called here. "What kind of a doctor was he?" she wondered. A little later, on a brand new page of her notebook, she would let her imagination guide her towards the answer.

"The doctor is on his way, Mrs. Gautier," whispered Sister Hélène. "He'll explain it to you."

Thérèse Gautier, her face hidden in her handkerchief, between two sobs, whispered: "Is he gonna save my Louis, at least? Eh, Sister, is he gonna save him?"

At that very moment, Doctor Thomas enters the small waiting room and sits on the wooden bench next to Mrs.

Gautier.

"Mister Gautier is a lucky man. What at first looked like tuberculosis is simply an acute bronchitis. I'll save your husband, Mrs. Gautier," the doctor said quickly and gently, "but you're going to have to take good care of him," he said, taking her hand in his. "Otherwise...I'm not responsible for what happens."

"Thank you! Oh thank you, Doctor!" cries Thérèse, "I'll take good care of him, for sure. You'll see."

But that is exactly what worries the doctor. "For months I've been trying to get through to these mothers that they are killing their husbands and children by overheating their houses, never letting in the fresh air, keeping them in the kitchen for hours near the coal stove until they are turning scarlet!" he had complained, again and again, to his wife.

"Your husband needs to rest for a few weeks. Then he should go outside, Mrs. Gautier—dressed warmly of course! He has to get some fresh air. It's very important."

"But Doctor, that's how he caught cold!"

"On the contrary! He is having trouble breathing and his lungs are tired because he has been sitting at home in the heat, doing nothing. He needs fresh air and exercise," the doctor adds, trying to sound authoritative, but is just barely convincing. "If you want him to be able to go back to his fishing in the spring, you'll have to listen to me on this one…"

He feels his instructions carry some weight. The work argument is more persuasive than all his theories about fresh air and exercise, which he knows confuses his patients and their families. According to an old local saying that people would not stop repeating to him, a draft that is not strong enough to blow out a candle is still strong enough to kill a man.

Mrs. Gautier stands up.

"Can I go and see him?" she asks.

"Certainly. We'll keep him here a few more days and then he can go home. Go ahead."

After Mrs. Gautier leaves, Doctor Thomas goes back to his office. He thinks about the numerous patients upstairs in the sanatorium, fighting their disease, alone, away from their loved ones. Some days he observes the patients who are still strong enough to stand at the window, to "watch life go by," as they say, or wait for a member of their family to come by and from the street shout the latest news from their child, their mother, their grandfather.

He feels desperately inadequate in his struggles against the disease which he fights without much success most of the time. "Such misery! On the sea, on the land, in their homes...everywhere, illness and accidents afflict these poor souls. I see nothing but suffering, from morning to night."

All the trusting expressions on the faces of his patients and their families affect him deeply. "They look at me as though I can do anything. And I know so little..."

"Doctor, Doctor, come quickly! Marie-Marthe Puchuluteguy is about to deliver her baby," explains Sister Hélène, utterly flustered. "It's a breech birth..." she adds, with a worried look.

One day, Émilie studied and then put aside the photographs taken at sea or onboard fishing boats. A sailor's daughter, she could appreciate the sailboats, three-masters, brigs, and schooners cutting a fine figure on the banks. But aside from the boats themselves, she could find nothing that connected the photos to the islands. On the other hand, she liked to look at every little detail of the ones taken on the decks of fishing boats. These ones reminded her of the working class world of Émile Zola's novels, which were taught in high school that year. Although there were no mines or shantytowns in the photos, the scene was just as sad: The men, overworked, dirty, freezing cold (it was easy to tell), were catching, splitting, and cleaning the cod.

"How did the doctor manage to take such clear shots when he was standing on the deck of a boat in constant motion, and with everything going on around him?" she asked Jacques, after she had shown him the series of photos.

"And what was he doing on a boat, anyway?" she added.

Other shots showed the ships in the Saint-Pierre harbour, while the fish were being taken off the boats and weighed. One in particular fascinated her. Cod was piled on a scale, and all around stood the men who had loaded it. There was salt everywhere: on their clothes, in their scruffy beards, on the deck. The photo was the colour of a shroud, allegory of death, faithful companion of the Terre-Neuvas as they sailed the seas. Suddenly, rather than Zola, the image brought to mind passages from *Pêcheur d'Islande*, a novel she had read a few years ago. She realized that the author, despite her earlier impressions, had not exaggerated anything. Would François like this photo? She could not decide right away, so she put it to one side. She remembered what her grandmother often used to tell her: "We are here only because of the cod. Everything that happened was related to it. Lucky for some, unlucky for others. In Saint-Pierre, just like in Miquelon, the meaning of our life has always been fish...fish and nothing but fish."

She began a new pile next to the pile of rejected photos, which she would have to look at again later. Time was running out. The end of the school year was just around the corner, and her family would be going to Langlade for the summer holidays. She would only be back in Saint-Pierre at the beginning of September, right before school started again. The family wanted to make the most of the summer paradise.

Already, preparations were underway. There was only one way to get to Langlade, a weekly mail boat that brought the supplies: bread, meat, fresh fruit, and vegetables. For the common necessities, they had to plan and pack carefully, so they would not find themselves missing something essential. You did not want to start making a cake only to realize you did not have enough sugar, look for pasta to eat with your ham and find only alphabet soup noodles, or even worse, get a picnic basket ready for the mid-afternoon snack and notice that there were no teabags or cans of milk left. It was a bit shameful to have to go to your neighbour's—who, like the ant in La Fontaine's fable, had never been caught "without"—to borrow a cup of sugar, a box of noodles, or a dozen teabags. And then you had to contact the grocer in Saint-Pierre and give him the grocery list so that you could replace the items from the neighbour's pantry as quickly as possible. The neighbour would give you an indulgent smile that seemed to suggest she was thinking how badly organized the family was.

Having experienced this many times in the past, Mother and Grandmother tried harder every year to better prepare their supplies, and filled every box they could find—empty crates of condensed milk, Sunkist oranges, Johnny Walker whisky—with supplies, tied them up neatly, and stored them in the entryway. The pile was getting higher every day.

Sardines in oil and Géo brand pâté for picnics; boxes of soup mix for busy evenings; sauerkraut, blood pudding, and wieners to have on hand for the tropical storms that occurred after August 15, and that prevented the mail boat from delivering the provisions; a big tin full to the brim with Milady brand English toffees (which Émilie took large handfuls of and shared with her friends); and Poulain brand chocolate bars she stuffed in a pocket of her backpack, along with two chunks of baguette, when she went swimming in the Belle Rivière. All these preparations usually filled her with happiness, and she could not wait to be on her way. This year, however, she barely noticed the activity. She had not yet finished choosing the photos and would be away for two months.

"Don't worry," the photographer said. "It'll give me time to sort out the rest of the plates. When you come back, you'll have a better selection."

His reasoning did not manage to convince her. In her race toward the finish line, she began to spend every moment of her spare time in the studio.

"I've been thinking," the photographer announced to her one day. "Why don't you take the photos of Miquelon-Langlade with you? I've just finished printing them. Once you're there, you can sort them."

Standing with the wind blowing in her face, her knees rocking in harmony with the waves, Émilie watched as the coast of Langlade emerged on the horizon and then hid behind the slightly dishevelled fog banks hanging onto the crests of the waves in the middle of the bay. A little further out—she could tell by the mild temperature of the air that caressed her face and the brightness in the west—the fog was going to disappear all of a sudden, leaving the sunshine in its place filling the air with its glittering reflections, dancing gleefully on the waves, and setting the quartz cliffs of Langlade alight. Indeed, a few minutes later, on the deck, the passengers opened up their pea jackets or oilskin coats to take in the welcome rays of sunshine. Voices became louder, as people knew they no longer had to keep the silence mandatory in the fog, which allowed the captains to hear the sound of the surf that announced the coast only a few minutes before they landed, or the approach of another craft also blinded by the fog and risking a collision. The use of radar in the mail boat had done nothing to change this reflex, which had been reinforced by centuries of "Hush!" "Be quiet!" "Shut up!" or "Listen," repeated by the captains who knew they could never be too careful.

This is the way the *Saint-Eugène* sailed into the Langlade summer, around the Anse-aux-Soldats. Well protected from the coast, the boat stopped moving; the hunting dogs tied to the rail that had moaned and groaned from the time they left Saint-Pierre now calmed down, feeling the inshore breeze. The poor people who had suffered from seasickness could now relax, happy to have refrained, by sheer will power and concentration through-out the entire crossing, from heaving their breakfast into the ocean, though it had been calm this morning.

For Émilie, summer began with this familiar ritual that never bored her. As soon as the steam pushing the boat ahead died down, and the boat began its graceful slide into its moorings, it signaled for her a slower, gentler pace of life.

The dune stretched out straight ahead of her. To the

left above the pebbles of the shoreline was the mouth of the Belle-Rivière. Further back, at the edge of the woods, the little red and white chapel hailed its parishioners. Here, even religious ceremonies were lighter. On Sunday they gathered at the chapel at the convenience of the priest from Miquelon or the one from Saint-Pierre, whenever they could get a "lift" in a vacationer's dory or some other vessel. "What time is Mass?" people would ask, on the road to the farm. If no one managed to find out, they would keep an eye on the activity around the summer camp and the chapel...Sometimes they simply waited for the first person to arrive to ring the church bells. The parishioners would sit cheerfully in the tiny chapel, trying not to make the old wooden pews creak as they sat down, and would delegate the duties: "Who wants to read the Scriptures?" "Do you want to take the collection?" "How about the offertory?" Everything in Langlade required collaboration, whether it was in the chapel or on the beach, where the men were clustered right now, rolling up their sleeves and in their waders, as they waited for the dories full of supplies and passengers to help unloading.

In her little suitcase, safely tucked in a plastic bag to keep them out of harm's way (sometimes packages fell into the water between the ship and the dory when they were unloaded), she had carefully (and secretly) packed Doctor Thomas' photos to bring them back to the place where they had been taken. Émilie choked up at the thought. She had not even had a chance to look at them, since Jacques had finished printing them just before she left.

"Keep it as a surprise for when you get to Langlade," Jacques had suggested the night before. "That will be even better! And enjoy your summer. You've got plenty of time; François won't be back until fall."

Standing on the shore amidst the ruckus, Émilie started collecting her things, the way everyone else was doing, to find the crates and the suitcases that belonged to her family in the clutter of packages and containers of all sorts: Robin Hood flour bags full of weekly bread supplies (six baguettes, three one-pound loaves of bread, four three-pound loaves, two thinner baguettes, and four loaves of sliced bread), pots of paint and cans of nails, piles of wood and roof felting to repair the summer homes. To her great relief, she saw her suitcase and hurried to put it in safety above the high-water mark, before she went to give her mother a hand carrying everything to Mr. Olivier's trailer. Every year Olivier, the only farmer in Langlade, who was also the radio operator, the postmaster, and the makeshift mayor in this paradise without a government, kindly delivered their "move" to the foot of their property on his way back home. At the end of the day, when most of their things were put away, Émilie's mother would open the garage doors and try to get the old jeep started.

Since arriving in Langlade, Émilie had slowed down even more, the way one might expect when people are on holidays. She never accepted the farmer's offer to drive her to their place; instead, she happily set out on foot along the dirt road. She needed to walk, at least the first time she went to the house every summer. The smell of manure, seaweed, and firs was intoxicating. The road, its surface a patchwork of potholes and cow dung, imprinted the irregular and deep rhythm of nature on the soles of her feet as she walked, and she found this made her feel good after the endless artificial flatness of the paved streets. The straps on her backpack weighed heavily on her shoulders, her feet overheating in her rubber boots, and sweat dripped down her back under the heavy sweater and yellow oilskin that were part of the uniform of travelling Langlade citizens. But it did not matter. She felt as light as a soul floating towards happiness. *Did the doctor feel this way when he landed here?* she wondered.

She was delighted to be in her room again with its pleasant musty smell and a faint odour of grass and sand as well. Her back was warmed by the heat beginning to penetrate the roof felting, which in August would make her refuge in the attic stifling. She opened her suitcase and took out the envelope of photos, which she stuffed under her pillow, along with her diary, until she could find a minute alone to freely look at them. Her mother was already calling her to take care of some necessary chores: go and get water, bring in the wood to make a little fire, and get rid of the humidity that lingered after the full yearly cleaning her father had done the week before.

Langlade belonged to the women of the family. Her father hardly had time to visit in the summer; he would take a week or two of holidays at most. However, before they got there he made sure everything was in working order: took off the shutters that protected the windows, removed the cowl at the top of the chimney, and primed the pump. Then he got the twelve-volt generator going, charged the batteries, and started the gas refrigerator stored in the little shed behind the house that made it possible to keep the meat cold a little longer than in the old days. They could even make delicious ice cream.

Émilie and her mother shared the rest of the chores,

but it was little enough for the privilege of being able to call Langlade home for two months, to have an immense playground with limitless possibilities for games to invent.

At the end of the day, the cardboard crates had disappeared into the shed; the suitcases had taken up residence under the beds; the pantry shelves were warping under the provisions; the stove, which had been on all day, had got rid of the humidity; and the kettle was singing—all signs that summer had begun.

By dusk, all the chores were done and Émilie took the envelope of photos and walked up the hill behind the house. This little mound in the middle of the woods had been her spot since childhood. Here she had played enjoyable games of Cowboys and Indians with her friends. And now, sitting on the headland and looking out to the isthmus of Langlade and, beyond that, Miquelon, she became reacquainted with her paradise.

In a second, painlessly, seamlessly, she felt free from the sadness that invaded her so often. She no longer felt muddled, anxious, doubtful. Here, everything was in its place. "Even me," she mused. She had always felt this way; she had often noticed that when she was in Langlade she wrote much less. Not because she did not have the time, but because she was at peace with the world around her and depended less on her pen to deal with everyday life.

The isthmus, the ocean, the hills of Miquelon, the mouth of the Goulet that she could make out in the distance, had been there for centuries, unchanged. "This is what Jacques Cartier saw when he came in 1534," her grandmother, a history buff, reminded her sometimes. Langlade never allowed itself to be put to shame and, with a minimum of effort, it accepted you as you were, asked nothing in return except for mutual respect. Émilie remembered that when she was a child, upon their arrival in Langlade, she would put on her pyjamas early in the evening, much to her mother's dismay since she knew Émilie would be out playing for hours yet, skipping rope with her friends or running after the cows set free to wander after the evening milking. Much later, Émilie understood that by getting ready for bed so early in the evening, she was trying to trick fate. In her child's mind, once she was in her pyjamas, there could be no question of going back to Saint-Pierre.

She had long ago abandoned this ruse, but she still felt a need to perform a ceremony to mark their arrival. On top of the hill, she could reconnect herself to Langlade, like the bushes and dwarf pines that surrounded and protected her. She occupied only a tiny place, a place that was hers alone, and she felt as if she was part of the nature around her, just like these twigs, this mushroom, or this fern. After all, some parts of nature disappeared in the fall and returned in the spring, did they not? The Langlade people who came from Saint-Pierre at the beginning of July were a little like annuals, blooming in this paradise.

When Émilie was on this hill—a fort made of brambles and firs tucked away and hard to find for anyone unfamiliar with all the small paths that wound their way through the alder trees, camouflaged by the tentacles of roots and branches—anything could happen. She was sheltered from the world. At worst, if her fort was invaded or she needed to escape, she could hide or even disappear. When she was little she often imagined the worst case scenarios: war was declared, Saint-Pierre invaded. An enemy contingent tracked them down in Langlade but were back on their way shortly afterwards, unable to find them on the mountain. Here, nothing bad could happen to her.

It was reassuring for her to be here, even today. She leaned up against a large rock, deposited there, her mother had explained, by an advancing glacier millions of years ago. This image usually made her think about the immensity of time, but today her mind was elsewhere, on the envelope of photos she had just placed on her lap.

The first picture made her smile. You could see the high tide mark where she had landed that very morning. The mail boat, an old tub, was moored to the same buoy while the Cap aux Morts rested at the back to the left. The same pebbles, the same waves, the same perspective. For Jacques Cartier, as well.

Doctor Thomas was as careful with the composition as he was with capturing his memories. He had positioned a woman and a little girl beside a man with a big belly and a thick moustache that seemed to hide a mischievous smile. She had seen him before…Let's see…Yes, Mr. Larranaga, a Basque farmer whose farm was located in the middle of the isthmus. It had long since disappeared, but she recognized him from her grandfather's photos. If seeing this rather rustic man made her smile, it was because he was famous in her family for his rough French.

"Mister Larranaga was married several times," her grandmother told her, always with the same pleasure, "three times, in fact. His last wife had been married once before as well. People died young in those days," she added, so people would not think these two valiant people were fickle or that they married on a whim. "And each couple had children. That made quite a gang of sons and daughters, and when people asked Mister Larranaga who was the father or mother of one of the children, he would always answer: 'All this, our children.'" It was a sweet little anecdote which, along with the photo, took on a special flavour. *After all,* Émilie often thought while she listened to her grand-mother's anecdotes, *that's history too.*

Turning back to the photo, she guessed that the two other people must be the doctor's wife and daughter. What the woman next to the farmer was wearing did not look like Mrs. Larranaga's clothing; she was accustomed to working hard on the farm, and along with taking care of the animals, the yard, and the kitchen, she was famous for having saved people from certain death on the dune in winter after a shipwreck—and more than once. In the photo, everyone looked happy: the passengers, glad to arrive in Langlade, no doubt, and the farmer to be in such pleasant company. Émilie was happy herself, pleased to see that summers in Langlade had not changed.

"You stand there, Mister Larranaga. And you too, Marthe," the doctor said to his daughter, who was already busy throwing pebbles in the water.

The farmer, proud as a peacock, stood up tall. He was being honoured by having his portrait done with the good doctor's wife and daughter. The hangers-on who filled the high-water mark that morning watched with interest and envy.

"Doctor Thomas and his family are on board. They are coming to the farm," the farmer had made sure to tell

everyone in sight that morning. He was making his way to the shore to await the little steamship that had just rounded the Cap aux Morts.

Smiling discreetly, the doctor contemplated the scene he had just composed. The atmosphere was one of simple happiness: the fair weather, the soft caress of the breeze in Marthe's and Emma's hair, the obvious pride of the farmer, who held his suspenders with his thumbs, the sparkling waves, the distant promise of the Langlade dune.

A childlike carefree pleasure came over him. The suffering of his patients, the odour of camphor and death vanished, the feeling of helplessness in the face of disease evaporated, his heavy responsibilities temporarily lifted... Today, between the salt air of the ocean and the softness of the meadow, the doctor thinks only of the pleasure of the carriage ride up to the Larranaga farm, the delicious meal promised by the generous farm-wife, the wild berries that would sweeten the dessert, the inimitable stories the farmer would tell...

"Don't move!" he said.

The first day of holidays was about to begin.

Émilie focused next on a series of photos featuring the doctor's wife and daughter: one of them horseback riding in the Goulet, with its singular contrast of the riders and black horses against the dazzling white-hot sand in the August sun; another of a dreamy-eyed rider in the foreground who had stopped at the site of a shipwreck run aground on the West dune. Émilie could tell it was the day after a storm because she could see the disorderly waves of a sea that had not yet recovered from its fit of rage. All of the photos had been taken in the summer.

You had to be intimately connected with the landscape to recognize the season. On this isthmus, windswept just about every day of the year, summer could be distinguished by some sparse and thorny plants that managed to survive in a few of the most sheltered spots. It could be felt more than seen, in the softer surf, in the glow of the sun high above the idling waves, in the green patches around the tolts at Delamaire's place, in the absence of snow on the hilltops in Miquelon. Things that would matter little to a tourist, but to the initiated, meant everything.

She thought that the photos would please François, that they would bring into his office in Paris a little bit of the ocean, a gust of iodine-scented sea air from Langlade, *a little bit of happiness*, she thought, having always suspected he missed it terribly. Just as she did.

Then she looked at the photos Doctor Thomas had taken when he was out hunting, and one in particular stood out, with dozens of Canada Geese with their immaculate bodies and their long black necks that stood like exclamation points of pain on the snow. A hunting companion of the doctor's, dressed in white, was parading in front of his victims, proud of having managed to trick them and kill them, despite the fact that they "usually took wing when they heard the hunter shoulder his rifle." That's what her Uncle Louis, who loved hunting migratory birds, had told her, sighing with regret at the thought that he had never been able to put a feather of one of these birds in his cap.

She put that snapshot aside, despite herself. François liked hunting. It was a way for him to feel like a local son who had grown up here and still belonged here in spite of having gone away to school at a very early age, and never staying for more than a few weeks since then, his father having died before he had taught him to hunt. Émilie understood that he had started hunting late in life, having learned to do it so he could join his brothers and friends on common ground.

He would no doubt like the idea of hanging this image—so incongruous in Paris—on the wall of his office, if only to be able to see the reaction of his visitors.

As the sun slipped down into the west, she hurried to leaf through the rest of the snapshots, all similar to the first ones—except for the very last one.

She immediately recognized the place although it was taken in the middle of winter (February, she guessed) in Miquelon. It was a picture of Cap Blanc taken from the top of a hill: *the Chapeau, perhaps*, she thought, trying to orient herself. It was not easy, given the lack of landmarks in the picture. It did not really show anything else except an expanse of snow-covered barrens and glacial rocks that had come to rest at the edge of the leaden ocean, motionless and colourless. It was as if nature had been frozen in time, the Earth had stopped turning, and the Moon had fled, taking the tides with her. Émilie shuddered, although she could not help but appreciate the indescribable beauty of the sunset, which at this very moment, to her left, beyond the West dune, had set the isthmus ablaze like a *toro de fuego* on Bastille Day.

This Miquelon was foreign to her. Since she only came to Langlade in the summer, she had no idea what her paradise was like in its winter garb. She did not know where the snow likes to hide, where the snowdrifts pile up like sand dunes, where the wind stings the most sharply, or where the blustery wind erases the roads, hides the paths, and blinds the most hardy of men. Was it possible that the panorama that caressed her this very moment, with all its soft curves and copper-coloured highlights, could turn into this disembodied spectre later in the season? How could nature be both so warm and so glacial?

And why had the doctor climbed the hills that day, in such uninviting weather? What had he seen in this grey and black panorama? She thought the photo was superb in its stark beauty and tried to imagine the photographer's state of mind when he stood behind his camera. What distress had led him there, to be captivated by this cruel and sublime beauty? What spirit moved him to transform such a bare landscape into such poignant beauty?

Three

By the time she returned from Langlade in September, Émilie had chosen the prints she considered the most representative of Doctor Thomas' body of photographic work in Saint-Pierre et Miquelon.

"Look," she told Jacques. "I've put together pictures of Saint-Pierre, the work on the beach, the mariners' celebration, the ice-cutting on Frecker pond—I didn't even know they used to do that! There are also photos of the ocean, of the cod being weighed onboard a banker, of French schooners on the Grand Banks, and of course lots of landscapes. And the photo of the doctor on the ice floe by the island: It was the first photo you showed us last winter, remember? Then some of horseback riding in the Goulet, of shipwrecks on the West dune, fields on the Larranagas' farm...And just to please François, I decided to add one taken after a trip to hunt the Canada goose and one hunting seabirds from a dory in Miquelon."

Jacques nodded his head in approval, impressed

by the impact the photos had when they were all put together. Set apart from the collection he had processed, they revealed the soul of their creator. He found it very powerful.

"And to finish it off, I put in these two," she continued, "one of Cap Blanc in the winter and one of the doctor sitting on a capstan, holding a seal in his arms."

"They stand out from the rest of the collection, don't they?" Jacques asked.

"Yes, but it seems to me that the starkness of nature in the photo of Cap Blanc is something like the attitude of the doctor himself, sitting there in his oilskins on the capstan, expressionless and holding a seal. I think he looks troubled. Anyone else would be smiling, holding such a cute and harmless little animal. But not the doctor."

She suddenly remembered the piercing cries that young seals made in the summer on the sandbanks of the Goulet—shrieks that sounded like the cries of infants in distress—and wondered if the doctor had been troubled by this sound.

"Everything is here!" Jacques declared, proudly.

"Why do you say that?" she asked, curious to hear his professional opinion.

"We can feel the complexity of a man torn between his daily work and his ideals. Despite his reputation as a doctor and the respect with which he was probably treated, the poor man seems to have gone from smile to despair. Look at the contrast, for example, between the photo of Cap Blanc, which is like a heart-wrenching cry from a desperate artist, compared to the horseback ride in the Goulet, the very image of carefree harmony. See what I mean?"

"That's exactly what I thought!" she exclaimed.

"So, is the work progressing? I'll be there soon, you know," François announced at the other end of the line.

She could sense his impatience. He was somewhere in North America, in Washington, she thought she had heard. To be honest, she had not really paid attention; she was completely caught off guard by his voice. She loved the intonations that were so typical of him, the warm tone of his voice, the spontaneity that moved her each time, especially since she knew how more restrained he was in his working life. He had only to utter a word or two for her to be able to see him as clearly as if he were right beside her.

This time he was calling from nearby, he explained. Somewhere in America, in a four-star hotel, in a huge room that was neutral to a fault, totally impersonal, with two big double beds. It could just as easily be in Tokyo, Singapore, or Berlin. How many times had he woken up in the middle of the night in a hotel room, feeling totally disoriented and not knowing where he was? However, tonight he felt close to the people he loved. At least a thousand kilometres, as the crow flies, separated them, but even so, because they were on the same continent, with an hour and a half time difference, it seemed to him that he was breathing their air and feeling the same Atlantic breeze on his cheeks.

As they approached North America, François had felt rather than seen a patch of his islands under the clouds. He always insisted on booking a window seat, and halfway over the ocean he would begin searching the horizon. First he watched for the coast of Newfoundland to slowly emerge. The island had plenty of rocky cliffs and mountain peaks, but seen from high above, he could barely see it emerging out of the waves. An immense landmass, where lakes, rivers, fjords, and bays seemed to overtake the rocks, peat, and heather, Newfoundland looked like a sponge soaked in water doing its best to float on the surface of the ocean.

He plunged back into a familiar universe. He tried to identify the coast that was visible, to make out, in the lunar landscape, the minuscule communities hugging the cliffs as tightly as they could, to get even closer to the cod. A few years earlier, during a trout fishing expedition on the southern coast of Newfoundland, he had seen these villages, without streets, isolated from everything and sometimes built directly on the water, houses perched up on stilts, straddling the coast and the wave, like modest Venices of the north where dories were used as gondolas.

The architect had been mesmerized by the ingenious skill of people who were ready to make any sacrifice in order to pursue their trade as fishermen. He had also realized the size of the material gap between the residents of Saint-Pierre et Miquelon and Newfoundlanders. Aside from a few fishing shanties at the tip of Savoyard or the Allumette Cove, which were used a few days every summer, no one on the French islands lived in such precarious conditions.

His nose pressed up to the window, he kept watch for the islands, for the moment (rather unpredictable, since the route changed often) when the coast of Newfoundland disappeared and made way for the islands. He crossed his fingers that no clouds would get in the way, because they could be seen only for a fleeting moment. First the cape of Miquelon emerged, then the dune of Langlade, and the lighthouse at Pointe Plate; if he was sitting on the other side of the airplane, it was Saint-Pierre and the minuscule Île-aux-Marins that came into view.

He had just enough time to look at his tiny "rock," to feel a tug on his heart as he looked for Voiles Blanches, Anse aux Soldats, Savoyard, all the places he loved, and to catch, on a sunny day, the reflection of a window being closed by a schoolteacher at the end of the day or by a government messenger delivering a notice to the *Conseil Général* officials. It was like a friendly wink to him, thirty thousand feet above. Then there was nothing until they flew over the coast of Nova Scotia. It was a moment of eternity though. All his life, the lives of his ancestors, his family, his friends, Jacques, Émilie, all his memories, his experiences, his favourite places: They were all condensed in these few minutes during which he could contemplate, and in a single glimpse, his islands.

This time, like every other time, he felt torn and could think of nothing else when he arrived in the United States, until he could find a telephone.

It was Émilie who answered. He was hoping that would be the case and had calculated the time difference so that she might still be home by herself, that they could have a chance to talk about everything and nothing, the photos, the doctor, school and her classes, the weather, anything at all as long as they could get as close as possible, and feel, temporarily, some comfort in their closeness.

In October, François set the dates for his trip. Jacques

hurried to finish printing the photos Émilie had chosen and get ready to showcase them.

"We'll have to hang them somewhere," Jacques decided. "That way François can really appreciate them. They're so beautiful."

"You haven't really got the room, though."

"No, that's true. We'll have to find some other spot. Let me think about it."

A few days later, Jacques went to see his friend Edmond, a former businessman who had retired a long time ago and who was passionate about the history of Saint-Pierre et Miquelon. A few other people as enthusiastic and determined as he was joined him in setting up a museum to preserve the local heritage. Government officials seemed to be as indifferent to these antiquities as the population was. "Chrome table mentality," Edmond muttered disdainfully each time someone reported that an oak bed had been burned at the city dump, or that a vacant house on the Île-aux-Marins had been pillaged by tourists who knew the value of the "old junk" contrary to the indifferent heirs who had abandoned it. He struggled ardently against this affliction, and was known for his outbursts.

Edmond dealt with all the decisions of the Friends of the Museum, all the serious issues, all the political games, artfully and with good humour; he was highly skilled at getting what he wanted. Matters were dealt with at his house, in his living room with a glass of scotch before dinner. Edmond went out once a day, cane in hand, to take a walk, but he never visited anyone. Whatever the circumstances, people came to him. He held a Salon every evening at six-thirty, and with the help of a bottle of Black & White they brought from time to time, his regulars made themselves at home. His wife discreetly served the more delicate souls some Saint-Raphaël or some port.

So it was in these chambers, which housed the leaders in the domain of heritage preservation of the islands, that the photographer came to discuss Doctor Thomas' work and the series of prints he had just finished. He did not say a word about Émilie's involvement in the project. She had confided that she preferred to stay in the shadows for the time being. But he explained the problem: Where was he going to be able to exhibit such a fine collection so that his famous purchaser could see it in its best light?

"In the museum," replied Edmond, putting down his glass of scotch long enough to light a cigarette. "In the museum," he repeated emphatically.

"You have no more room in your museum than I have in my shop!" retorted Jacques, with a smile.

"Well, we'll just have to move something then. And anyway," he added, not one to miss an opportunity, "it would be good to give everyone a chance to see these photos. They deserve it. Would you let us have them for a week or two?"

"You know very well we have far too many things in the museum already, Edmond," said an old lady who seemed to be lost in the big armchair next to his, but whose fragile physical appearance hid an iron will.

"Oh, we'll find a way, Henriette," Edmond replied. "We always do, you know." He directed a complicit wink her way.

Henriette had supported him since he first started talking about the museum. A retired schoolteacher, exceptionally gifted with the French language and blessed with limitless curiosity, she had taken upon herself to search the archives for historical documents. She had found some, in terribly bad condition, that had been put on the floor of the basement in the government building to sponge up water after the flood, as the janitor who opened the door for her so she could begin working explained to her, clearly seeing nothing wrong with it.

It was Henriette who, in her name and Edmond's, had written numerous letters to politicians asking them to find a place to house the museum. And again, it was Henriette who had convinced the local population to share and display their souvenirs. A few announcements in the "Local Notices" on the radio, which they all listened to religiously at noon before the news, was all it took. Between "For sale: two-year-old puppy" and "The Gaspard family is pleased to announce the birth of their daughter..." the idea of a museum had taken hold.

The governor had come for a before-dinner drink— followed by the mayor, the senator, the member of parliament, the chair of the *Conseil Général*—all suddenly committed to protecting the history of their forefathers and all eager to be named as founders of the museum. As far as the population was concerned, people were thrilled to show off their family heirlooms and, in some cases, to get rid of them without having to make a trip to the dump. In any case, they answered the call and came with their wooden clogs, their compasses, old photos, rosary beads, Jesus of Prague miniatures, old coins from the Napoleon period, oars, and killicks.

"But how are we going to find room for them?" Henriette mused.

"Let's see," said Edmond.

Silence reigned for a few moments while everyone

pictured the museum in their minds. It was situated on the third and top floor of one of the oldest buildings in Saint-Pierre. Anyone who managed to make it to the top of the endless staircase, out of breath, was offered an interesting choice: to the left was the museum and to the right was the library, which would have been equally at home in the museum given that some of the books were old enough to have been handed down from Antiquity. Although there were still some empty shelves in the library, the museum gave the impression of being about to explode. *A real mess*, Jacques had often thought.

Across from the front door was a hallway lined with an eclectic collection of objects. On one wall were fishing tools, displays of mariner's knots, family trees of the Vigneau or Poirier, the Acadian families who had settled on the islands; on another, there were photos of schooners and a collection of war decorations. The whole thing was a whirlwind of information that visitors tried their best to grasp.

The corridor led to a little room in which stuffed samples of the island's fauna were displayed: snowy owl, spotted owl, silver fox, rabbit and partridge, snipe and geese, all looking more real than nature. In the showcases, slivers of rocks reminded the viewer of the geological origins of the islands. In short, this was the natural history section to which had been added, for want of an herbarium, an original copy of an herbal guide, *La flore laurentienne*, by Brother Marie-Victorin, an eminent Quebec botanist whose studies of the flora of eastern Canada described in minute detail the plant life of Saint-Pierre et Miquelon.

When visitors could no longer bear the glassy-eyed and, it seemed, reproachful looks of the fox and its cohort, they moved into the *pièce de résistance*, the room that contained the most precious objects: original manuscripts dating from the return of the islands to France in 1816—"For the last time," Henriette repeated tirelessly, to remind people that the history of Saint-Pierre et Miquelon consisted of unending battles between France and England. "Our islands were set on fire seven times," she would add emphatically. Next to these documents was prominently displayed something that looked like a deformed cannon ball, but it was actually the melted remains of the church bell of the first church in Saint-Pierre, destroyed in 1902 by a violent fire. And nearby was the head of Christ on the cross, a wooden sculpture that obviously belonged to a roadside Calvary: Years standing in the headwinds, and slapped by salt fog, had given the divine face a colour that was doubtlessly similar to Christ's own after his long agony on Mount Golgotha. To this odd assortment were added a few naive paintings by the only known artist of the islands, a Mr. Lemoine, vaguely remembered by a few elderly residents, and most of whose work had been rescued from attics and renovation projects since the museum had opened. Every centimetre of the wall was covered, and showcases filled all the remaining space. One display case contained a collection of bills from the CFA Bank. Jacques had no idea where there would be room for Doctor Thomas' photos in all this clutter.

"Move something, that's easy to say, Edmond," continued Henriette. "But you know very well that the collections are fragile. If we move them, we never know what might happen to them..."

Actually, the problem was that the museum, housed in a wooden building that was over a century old, had been overheated in the winter, the way all public buildings were, and in the summer had been left open to the attacks of the strong sunshine. This meant that the majority of items he was so determined to protect were slowly deteriorating.

"I know!" The voice came from a member of the inner circle who had been pensive up until that point. "We can take out the animals and the rocks. At least they'll have no trouble being moved."

"Marvellous!" cried Edmond. "The problem is solved."

Jacques did a quick mental calculation of the space that would be freed up by the removal of the taxidermy and geology sections. "That should do it," he concluded. "Thank you."

He decided not to ask where the wild animals, the quartz, and the granite would find a home.

The museum members got to work very quickly. Since there was no storage space in the museum, they divided the objects among themselves. The fox, the snipe, the goose, and the owl got a breath of fresh air as they were trotted over to somebody's house, while Brother Marie-Victorin's volume was returned to Henriette, who had lent it in the first place. The snowy owl, the partridge, and the Arctic hare took a little ride in the truck to a third member's house. The museum committee swept the floor clean and declared the room ready to present the photography exhibition that Edmond and Jacques had agreed to call: *The Islands of Doctor Thomas.*

This time François took the scenic route to get to his islands. Instead of going to Montreal, he landed in

Gander, in the middle of Newfoundland, rented a car—a big Impala—and drove to Fortune, a little village on the south coast, across from Saint-Pierre, where a little fishing boat was waiting to take him across to the islands.

The trip would give him a chance to make a gradual transition through time and space. The road to the Burin Peninsula, which normally took five or six hours in good weather, would do him good. It was certainly not the kind of paradise tourists with their Kodaks were after; the barrens stretched out as far as the eye could see, interrupted only by a few spindly fir trees that hinted timidly at the presence of a nearby stream. Other than that, there were enormous rocks—which François imagined had been abandoned by gods who had tired of their cosmic lawn bowling game—and a few puddles, tiny ponds. Peace.

After an hour or two, he could feel his stress disappear and his tired muscles relax, all the worries he carried with him every day vanish in this awesomely desolate landscape. Autumn was particularly well-suited to this part of the world, with its raw colours: In the refreshing, crisp air the blue of the sky turned cobalt in the ponds along the road, the heather like a fiery frame to the quartz glinting in the sun. There were no villages in this area. In fact, there was a section of the highway that went for almost a hundred kilometres without a single gas station. Here and there, highway signs announced the invisible communities of Grand-le-Pierre, Bay-L'argent, or Famine: "French names everywhere," his brother kept saying, "France was everywhere and it abandoned everything." A few cars passing in the other direction attested to the presence of these little hamlets close by, down a side road or up at a point.

By the time he got to Fortune, François had long ago discarded his identity of famous architect and put on the one that was much more comfortable, that of a local son, homeward bound. The sad fishing village with its tiny old-fashioned houses, its fish processing plant that spurted out pungent odours, with its narrow port where a few rusty trawlers, skiffs, and dories were moored—all of this seemed magnificent to him. With the confident stride of someone who loves the sea and who is eager to feel the rolling waves in his legs, François looked around for the friend who had been entrusted with the special assignment of bringing him home. As soon as he had found him, he handed the keys to the car rental agent, stowed his bag on the boat, and jumped in.

They reached Saint-Pierre during the night, at around eleven o'clock. The weather was so calm and the sky so clear that during the crossing he had been able to stand on the deck and look at the constellations, a rare treat for a city-dweller used to light pollution drowning out the power of the night. He could feel the iodine caresses of the sea breeze, a sign of welcome that touched him deeply. In the distance, muffled by the door of the wheelhouse that had been closed to keep the cool night air out, he could make out the conversations of a few crew members, who after a bit of small talk had left him alone on the deck. They could instinctively guess his need for solitude as he looked forward to his reunion with what they were lucky enough to call their everyday life.

Sitting by herself on a mooring buoy, Émilie watched the boat come into the harbour. You had to know where to look. She first picked out the light at the top of the mast as it slipped slowly into the roadstead, then down the Pointe aux Canons channel to the customs dock, before the boat appeared for a second in the projectors on the wharf. Her heart seemed to be racing even faster in the silence and solitude of the night.

The boat slipped into its regular place. In the lamplight of the wheelhouse she could see her father steering the vessel and make out a few other people, who were busy putting on their jackets and gathering up their luggage. She moved closer to the ship to catch the mooring line they were going to throw to her. At least that was her official reason for being on the wharf. She was in fact searching for François. She did not see him, she heard him.

"Hello."

He was leaning against one of the two dories tied to the rear deck, completely hidden by the darkness, at the exact place where, if she had been lucky enough to make the crossing on such a lovely night, she would have chosen to sit.

Pleased to surprise her, he climbed up the little ladder to the wharf and before anyone could set foot on land or come and interrupt them, he took her in his arms and held her for a moment, a more intimate gesture than any kiss could have been.

"So, it's done?"

"All done."

He loosened his grasp a little to let her see him, to get a good sense of his emotion. Then he leaned towards her and whispered in her ear, as if it were the most precious secret in the world.

"Thank you."

She could hear her father turn the engine key, a car stop on the wharf, the doors slam. François moved a few steps away, held her hand for a moment before letting go completely, and in a split second took on his role of local son. Only an hour before he had been convinced that he no longer had to pretend or prove anything when he was home.

"Thank you for picking me up," François said, before climbing into his brother's car. "See you tomorrow," he said to the little crowd, while still looking at Émilie.

The next morning, his first visit was to Jacques' studio. Émilie was in class, which annoyed him a little.

"So, where are these photos?"

The photographer smiled at his impatience.

"You wouldn't want to do that without Émilie, surely?"

François grinned like a naughty child who had been caught. Nonetheless, his eyes darted around the studio, hoping to find a pile of large-framed photographs.

"No use looking," teased the photographer. "Your photos are hanging somewhere where you can see them all properly. They are worth it, believe me. Émilie made a wonderful selection. In my opinion, she has impeccable judgment. It's impressive in someone so young," he added.

François listened to the photographer describe Émilie's qualities the way a father drinks in compliments about his daughter. He felt absurdly proud of her. Or was it of himself? Proud of having nurtured this tender bond between them instead of brushing it aside the way he usually did with his emotions.

"When are you planning to show them to me?" he asked, realizing that the stage had been set for a special event and he would not be able to escape from the performance.

"This afternoon at five o'clock. At the museum."

"The museum?"

"Don't worry, they made room. However, Edmond made me promise you would leave the photographs on display there for two weeks, so that the whole town could see them."

"Why not? Two weeks won't make much difference to me."

The photographer entertained him for a few more minutes by telling him the story of the trouble they had getting the photos up to the third floor, the debates about the arrangement and the order they should be put in, the height at which they should be hung, the captions that Émilie did not want to put on them so that François would discover each image the way she had. On that point, Jacques and Émilie had reached a compromise: The captions would be placed under each frame after his visit.

A customer came into the studio.

"A passport photo," the photographer whispered. "I have to go. Remember: five o'clock."

At five minutes to five, François arrived in front of the museum. He did not know if he should go in or wait outside. He was as nervous as a schoolboy, and felt ridiculous for being nervous. He waited a few more minutes, shook the hands of a few passersby, then decided to go up. Since there was no one in the hallway, he climbed the stairs as fast as he could in an attempt to relieve the stress. Émilie was already at the door of the museum. He could tell that she was as anxious as he was.

He gave her a kiss on each cheek, stepped back a bit, and then said, in an artificially casual tone: "All right, shall we go?"

"Let's go."

They were alone.

"Jacques will come a bit later. He had an appointment with a client," she explained.

François suspected it had more to do with discretion.

"And where are they, exactly?"

"In the natural history room."

Slowly, moving as if to make the most of their anticipation, they walked down the hall past the collections. Sometimes, to tease her, he would stop for a moment in front of some object, pretend to examine it, while looking at her out of the corner of his eye. She played along with a good-natured attitude, smiling in spite of her impatience so that he could tell she was not gullible. Total understanding even when playing games.

Finally they entered the room where the photographs were exhibited. It was the fruit of months of work, and she hoped it would be to his liking.

François was flabbergasted. The photos, which were superb, recounted without words the history of the islands and their people, their hard work and dedication, their rare moments of relaxation and enjoyment, the beauty of nature and also its cruelty. He was overcome by the strange sensation that there was something else underlying the photos. On the walls, he saw an expression of his own feelings, better than he could have expressed them himself. These images, captured by another man in another era, conveyed his sense of being torn and conflicted, the dissatisfaction with work despite success, the deep-rooted questions about the meaning of life, the feeling of never being completely at home...*All this in someone else's photos*, he thought.

Speechless, stunned, he moved slowly and silently from one frame to the next with Émilie at his side.

Everything was contained in these images: the happiness of simple pleasures and the pain they can cause, beauty and ugliness inextricably linked, emotion in the face of things that cannot be said, nostalgia for the past and the tensions of the present, the hidden sorrow, the ineffable distress in everyday actions. All these contradictions—his own as well as those of the artist—were obvious to him. They had been understood... no, the word was too weak...felt, grasped, both by the mysterious doctor and this young woman at his side who had chosen the images and therefore must also have felt the same tensions. He could not find any words to describe how he felt. It was skin deep, raw emotion. He finally found the courage to turn towards Émilie, who was waiting for his verdict, her heart in her throat, nervous. Moving away from these images that were such an accurate reflection of him, he said, "How did you do it?"

Not knowing what to say, Émilie shrugged and then made an attempt to explain. "First I tried to represent all the aspects of Doctor Thomas' work. But along the way I realized that my choices would illustrate his way of looking at things, at life, but also yours...and mine. I didn't set out to do it; I just followed my instincts..."

"It just happened, you mean."

"Yes. Because the project was for you. It's a little like

when you develop photos. First the images are invisible, then they're printed in negative, and finally they appear as they really are..."

"What I see is superb, and moving. Do you realize, Émilie, that we three, the doctor, you, and I, all see life differently than other people?"

She nodded.

"What a masterful achievement!" he exclaimed.

The photographs were a testimony to a complete communion of spirit, with no dark shadow or ambiguity, among three souls that everything separated, even death. "Finally!" he wanted to cry out. He took both her hands, drew her close and held her for a long while without moving or speaking. An inexplicable urge to cry came over him.

She smiled shyly at first. Then her eyes started to sparkle and her mouth opened into an irrepressible smile. Even though an instant ago he had been trying to repress his tears, and she was waiting in agony for his reaction, now they were both laughing, and hand in hand they went to look at the exhibition again from the beginning.

He wanted to know everything. Where had that photo been taken? When? Had she managed to identify the people in them? She answered his questions, explained a few of the difficult choices she had made, shared some of the details of her discussions with the photographer. The conversation was smooth and relaxed, in an atmosphere of total understanding and intimacy. In front of the photo of the doctor in Île aux Marins, François looked at Émilie, held her hand more tightly and murmured, "We have come a long way."

A few minutes later Jacques came in. They were all

smiles, standing in front of the photo taken after a goose hunting trip. "That one is definitely there to make you happy," Émilie told François. Behind their bursts of laughter an intense emotion lingered. *Mission accomplished, my dear*, thought the photographer, as he energetically shook their hands.

On his capstan, Doctor Thomas, his eyes staring out into space, just wanted to die.

Four

As he usually did when he came to the islands, François went to visit Émilie's parents the evening he arrived. He tried to communicate the depth and purity of the feeling that connected him both to their daughter and, across generations, to this doctor to whom she had introduced him.

He explained as best he could how it had happened: Last January they had crossed paths by chance, she had taken him to see the photographs Doctor Thomas had taken, and he had asked her to choose some of them for his office in Paris. Jacques had found them so beautiful that he had convinced Edmond to exhibit them in the museum before he took them back to France with him. Simple and true, although the most essential part was missing.

"Why didn't you tell us?" her parents asked, concerned that their daughter had hidden things from them.

"I was afraid I wouldn't be able to do it," she replied.

At best, her words were misleading, at worst, a lie. Although she had been afraid, for a while, that she would not have enough time to look at them all, she had never doubted her abilities. For him, she was capable of anything—that was the most magical thing about her bond with François. While she was often hesitant, tentative, uncomfortable in her everyday life, in this exceptional parallel life she lived, nothing prevented her from taking flight. But try making other people understand that! And all the more so your parents...

Émilie's parents accepted her explanations. They knew there was something else between their daughter and their friend that they could not grasp, a connection that escaped them. They were, however, sure that there was nothing to be worried about. Sometimes trust wins out over understanding. And they were very proud of their daughter.

The photography exhibit opened to the public with great pomp; Edmond did not want to miss such a perfect opportunity. Everyone rushed over to see it. Each image incited a treasure hunt in the town's collective memory. One person recognized a particular spot, another a schooner, still another could date the photo: "Look, it must have been after 1912; our house was already built." The older people recalled details they had believed long forgotten: the Légasse palace, the Boulot Bridge under the snow banks. The radio and television stations gave the event top billing on the local news reports. And of course, people swarmed to interview Edmond and Henriette, Jacques, and François.

François made sure he highlighted Émilie's role in the project, her careful choice and the challenges she had faced. Naturally, some wondered why he had entrusted the selection to a girl to whom he was not even related. He answered that question immediately, talking about the friendship that linked him to her parents and explaining that she had volunteered because he spent most of his time in France. The journalists then turned their attention to Émilie, which incited her classmates to call her arrogant.

"You know townspeople don't look kindly on people who stand out from the crowd," her father explained. "Everyone will be more than happy to tell people in France the story of the young girl who put together such a beautiful exhibition, but here, among ourselves, people will say she was just trying to be better than everyone else."

When they asked him about this important "first" for the museum, Edmond said he was thrilled about it, although he did add that "If we had a real museum, we could organize exhibitions like this more often. That would certainly be a good thing for the islands." The politicians seemed to take note of this. Henriette, for her part, stated that it was about time people showed some interest in the incomparable work of Doctor Thomas, and that she hoped he would be "discovered" in France. This time François took note.

Jacques was busy capitalizing on his success. Business was going swimmingly. Everyone wanted Doctor Thomas' photos. He sold them framed, as greeting cards, or simply prints for photo albums. They were spread in the homes across the island and around the world, given as gifts to expatriates or bought on visits home by people who no longer lived on the island but appreciated their little "rock," as they call their islands, with a sort of derision that often turns to melancholy. There was even talk of publishing a book of the best examples of Doctor

Thomas' work, a project the *Conseil Général* might fund in order to promote the islands.

However, the whole mystery of Doctor Thomas remained. Although the secrets behind his photos were being revealed, thanks to the memories of a few townspeople, the artist himself still hid in the shadows. Henriette had managed to track down some basic information about his visits to the islands. He arrived in 1912, left in 1914 (no doubt for the war), returned in 1915 and left in 1916—But why? He took a final trip in 1923, which lasted until 1926.

"Three trips for a military doctor is quite a lot," Henriette remarked.

"It is indeed," Edmond confirmed. "Generally a stay for a few years is quite enough. Even today," he added with sarcasm in his voice, "there are a few who want to leave as soon as they get here."

"Doctor Thomas must have loved the islands if he was so determined to be posted here," Henriette concluded. "That doesn't happen often."

In the days after the exhibition opened, François and Émilie had many opportunities to spend time together. She was even invited to cocktail hour at Edmond's. They served her Ginger Ale. Her exceptional parallel life was becoming real. There was so much to write about, to remember, to explain, to understand, and to immortalize that, for the first time since she had begun her diaries, she had to start a second notebook in the middle of the year.

Along with Jacques, they formed an odd trio, bonded together by a similar passion for Doctor Thomas and his work. Jacques feverishly set about printing the last few glass plates. Louis Thomas emerged from the shadows as quickly as his photos were printed. Everywhere people talked about him, came to see the exhibition of his photos, and hurried into the tiny studio to buy reproductions of them, glimpses into a life that had nearly fallen into oblivion.

"To think that such a beautiful building as Folquet's has disappeared," sighed an old fisherman. "The pebble beaches by Houduce's place were beautiful before they built the road along the shoreline," another viewer commented.

Suddenly, Doctor Thomas gave back to his Saint-Pierre audience their heritage when they came to admire his work: the reek of cod-liver barrels, the ancestral rhythms of the work of the sea, the splitting, washing, cleaning, drying, moving around the dried cod, putting the capelin in barrels, all the actions that islanders used to perform almost automatically but had now forgotten. He also gave them back their family and friends.

"Look, that's old man Sollier, there, showing the capelin drying."

"This is Larranaga, with his hands hooked into his suspenders. What a nice belly that is, eh?"

"And here," an old native of Dog Island said, "is Father Lavollée in front of the cross in the cemetery. Look, he's kneeling down, must be praying with Simone and Marie-Jo Lemétayer. Not sure who the other girls are."

"What's Father Lavollée like?" his wife asks him, curious, when he came home from one of his weekly trips to Dog Island.

In Saint-Pierre, everyone has heard about the priest on Dog Island, his sermons warning parishioners of the vices of Saint-Pierre society that were threatening to corrupt "his good island women" are legendary.

"My dear, I have to admit, he's a madman. There's no other word for him. In his opinion, women in Saint-Pierre don't know how to work. All they think about is having fun," the doctor sighs, thinking of all the women exhausted by their frequent pregnancies, the hard work of getting the cod ready, turning the soil in the garden, milking the cows, cooking the meals, washing the clothes, feeding the children...and who only go to the hospital as a last resort!

"Not like the good girls from his island?"

"Exactly. And that's not all! He's really worried about them...It's hard to believe, but the priest is horrified by the fact that there are girls and boys who hold hands when they skate on the pond. He says it's a scandal!" adds the doctor, half-amused and half-indignant.

"Oh, how very inappropriate, indeed!" his wife teases.

"But there's nothing to be concerned about, because good Father Lavollée has a solution for this scandalous behaviour. He even showed me his invention. It's a piece of wood about this long," explains the doctor, spreading his hands out in front of him, "with a place for the boy's hand on one side and the girl's hand on the other side. Incredible!"

"And what did you say when he showed you his marvellous invention?"

"Nothing. I just left. I would have said too much if I had stayed." He lets out an exasperated sigh. "You would think he had better things to do. Things are hard enough as it is."

The doctor seemed to be tickling the collective memory of Saint-Pierre from beyond the grave. Thanks to his photos, a wave of memories flooded the islanders' hardened minds. Jacques was moved by the sight of elderly people, sometimes leaning on a cane or the arm of a family member, who came into his studio to look at the albums. With their eye glued to the magnifying glass, they would add a new detail, sometimes insignificant but always interesting. Jacques was touched to see their gaze wander into the misty territories of their memory, hear the lump in their throat as they talked about having to come to terms with the cruel passage of time.

François and Émilie had noticed that Jacques often gave away copies of the snapshots to the old people who looked at them longingly.

"When they're living on their old age-pension, whether former workers or fishers, there's no way they can afford them," he said frankly.

One evening, Jacques, François, and Émilie decided to review the complete collection of photos, one by one, in order to organize them by theme, season, and place.

"So here's the final count: more than one thousand, two hundred," announced Jacques.

François should have made his way back to France—to his office, his plans, his tenders—but like an archeologist on a dig in a field of unexpected treasures, under no circumstances could he bring himself to miss these exciting moments. He had announced that he would return once the exhibition was over, which resulted in endless conversations with his partners. He began his third week in Saint-Pierre, and never had he been away from his office for so long.

"Are you sure this isn't going to cause problems?" his mother asked. She was always nervous about a boss becoming angry.

"Absolutely sure," he replied, with a smile. "I know because I'm the boss."

All of a sudden, this man, who took his responsibilities and his obligations so seriously, to the point that he sometimes forgot to take care of his most basic needs, realized that nothing could stop him from taking a break from his activities, that no one could say anything about it. He was entirely free to make his own decisions. A new serenity enveloped him.

For the moment, the most important thing was to get to work with his friend and for the doctor, and make sure the photographs did not end up making the Atlantic crossing by themselves. Nearly fifty years after they were taken, it seemed terribly important to François to correct the error the doctor had made when he left the islands and abandoned all the photographs without even trying (as far as he could tell, at any rate) to get them back.

"How could he have just left them?" he often said, looking at yet another striking view of life in Saint-Pierre et Miquelon.

It was still a mystery, even if the exhibition had at least enabled people to add a few details to the doctor's portrait. One person remembered he had seen the doctor walking on the mountain with his camera; another said he was a friend of Ernest Hutton's, the pharmacist, and that it was in Hutton's attic—"under the rafters" added the old man—that he had set up his darkroom. Mrs. Thomas was also remembered. She was a nurse.

"Mother went to see her just after I was born," explained a woman in her fifties. "Apparently, I cried all the time and Mrs. Thomas told her that her milk wasn't right for me." Interesting anecdotes, but they did not reveal any of the now-famous photographer's secrets.

Before hammering in the last nail in the crates he was shipping to France, Jacques had an idea: "What if we put the photos on display in Miquelon?"

"Miquelon?"

"After all, the doctor spent quite a bit of time there. And if we managed to find a place for an exhibition in Saint-Pierre, we'll certainly be able to find one there."

Miquelon, Saint-Pierre's sister island, had a population of seven hundred, eight times smaller than Saint-Pierre's. A boat ride there took only a few hours; still, it was as if the two communities were situated on opposite ends of the earth so completely different were their lifestyles and their mindsets.

Jacques, who had had a chance to spend several summers there as a child visiting relatives, had never figured out how two communities as isolated and tiny as Saint-Pierre et Miquelon could keep such a distance between each other.

"The photos will interest them just as much as us, maybe even more," he continued. "There's no reason not to go there, and if I lived in Miquelon, I tell you, I would be insulted if I weren't given a chance to see them."

"I don't see anything wrong with that idea," François said. Nonetheless, he was a bit disappointed he had not thought of it first. "What do you think?" he asked, turning to Émilie.

"I agree. We should have thought of that in the first place," she said, also feeling a bit guilty.

When an important event took place in Saint-Pierre—whether an artist's visit, a school project, or something else—there was rarely someone around to ask, "What about Miquelon?" The famous hospitality of the islanders did not seem to extend spontaneously to their neighbour island, and each island jealously kept its pleasures and treasures for itself.

Émilie was familiar with the difference between the islands because, every summer, her family crowded into the old Willis jeep for the long trip—twenty-five kilometres of dirt roads—from Langlade to the town of Miquelon.

"It's quite a trip!" she explained to them as she took the photos down from the walls of the museum.

The trip could only be made if the weather was right, if the weather report the night before promised one of those magical days without a cloud in the sky. This required a close examination of the weather patterns and the tidal calendar, complex calculations of the variables, and a determination of the probable time of the next low tide in the sound that needed to be crossed in order to get to Pointe au Cheval and the road to Miquelon. You had to already be there, ready to quickly cross the minuscule sound as soon as the ebb tide would allow it, cross over to Miquelon without delay, and then turn around and do the same thing in the rising tide.

It was generally best to go in the morning, and to travel as part of a convoy in case someone's vehicle broke down or got stuck in the sand. Two or three jeeps travelled the winding road along the beach and cleared a path through the little hills on the Delamaire farm and the Lamunth marshes. It took at least an hour to make it over the bumpy road. The passengers sang popular songs, which had the one redeeming value of making it easier to pass the time and help them forget the repeated jolts on their behinds.

When they got to the edge of the sound, they unpacked their picnic lunch. Depending on the tide, which they were able to judge with an experienced eye, they either rushed or took their time.

The sound was already Miquelon, or at least another world. Here, there were deer flies hiding in the grass, never seen on the eastern or the western dune. The water was both warmer and saltier than in Langlade, because it rose and fell in a little sandy lagoon where it had time to warm up in the sun all day long. On the other side of the sound, which Miquelon residents called a *barachois*, there were uncharted territories: bald hills, Île aux Chevaux, the Alouettes point.

At the appointed time, the convoy forged ahead, hugging the shoreline. In some places the sand under their wheels was firm, but in others they feared their vehicles would sink down into the sand; here, they sped ahead as fast as possible and made sure they did not have to break. Too bad for the passengers, who were thrown about. They finally reached the barrier of Pointe au Cheval, the official entry into Miquelon and where the Langlade folk officially became tourists, an impression that became stronger as they approached the town of Miquelon. It looked nothing at all like Saint-Pierre, where their town clung perilously to the side of a rock-face.

Miquelon was beautiful! Sprawled comfortably on a sandbank in the middle of the sea, a human challenge to nature because it was built on the most vulnerable location, at sea level, at the mercy of waves, nor'easters, and the raging sea on its western side. The steeple of Notre-Dame-des-Ardilliers Church rose proudly in the centre of a cluster of houses that were squatter and longer than those in Saint-Pierre, constructed in a way to block the ever-present wind. Spacious gardens lay on either side of the two long roads of the town; carrots, leaks, lettuce, and potatoes were planted there. That also differed from Saint-Pierre, where there was not much space, and family gardens were limited to a tiny plot between houses.

After running a few errands for their parents, the children would go to *Chez Rachel's* to buy cakes and sugar rolls. Rachel discreetly played the role of town baker, although she had no actual store, no front window or sign. Everyone knew where to find her though, and would make a beeline for her mocha cakes, cream puffs, and cake rolls. They would knock on her front door, saying, "Mama sent me to get some cakes," and Rachel, a short woman with round cheeks, curly hair, and a welcoming smile, would show them into her kitchen. On Sundays and holidays, there were cakes everywhere: baking trays covered in mocha cakes were placed on top of the gas stove, platters of sugar rolls nearly covered the dining-room table completely, and the unforgettable fragrance of butter, sugar, and vanilla floated throughout the entire house.

After enjoying Rachel's goodies, the young people wandered around town, on the Place des Ardilliers or visited the church, until their parents were finished shopping. Unlike Saint-Pierre's church, which was built of concrete and was vast and freezing inside, Miquelon's was made of wood, inside and out, and bathed visitors in its benevolent warmth. Light shone through the stained glass windows and illuminated a huge painting that filled the wall behind the altar—"a reproduction of Murillo's *Assumption*, given by Napoleon III as a gift to the people of Miquelon," her grandmother had told her. How had the Emperor of France found out about a church in faraway Miquelon? History did not bother explaining that part.

Late in the afternoon, the family stopped in "to say hello" to two elderly ladies her grandmother had known when she taught school in Miquelon. Then it was already time to leave, "if they didn't want to miss the low tide."

In the evening, after closing the gate at Pointe au Cheval behind the convoy, it felt as though they had returned from a vacation. When the wheels fell into the familiar tracks in the middle of the dune an hour later, it was as if the automobile could "smell the stable," as her father would say.

Her grandmother had a historical perspective—as she always did—on the strange phenomenon that distinguished the people of Saint-Pierre from those of Miquelon. The history of the two villages had been very different, despite their proximity. Miquelon had been settled by Acadians and a few opinionated Basques, Saint-Pierre by a wave of Breton, Basque, and Norman fishers, joined by a few "strangers," mostly from Newfoundland. In other words, Saint-Pierre's population was much less homogenous and more migratory than Miquelon's.

For almost a century, the psychological separation had kept the two communities apart, despite their geographical proximity—a distance of only a few nautical miles. The Acadians, with their tragic history of deportations, who were prevented from settling in

Saint-Pierre et Miquelon by a King of France reluctant to feed them, had learned to cherish their solitude.

The establishment of French communities on the islands had led to a demographic imbalance between them, and Miquelon had become the poor cousin, always the last to benefit from the generosity of their mother country. Even more than the isolation, this injustice, whether it was real or simply perceived, had separated them by a chasm that modern life had not managed to bridge.

The idea of breaking with tradition by taking the Doctor Thomas exhibition to Miquelon pleased all three of them.

"Let's go over before I leave," François suggested.

The longer his stay in Saint-Pierre lasted, the more impatient his partners in Paris were getting. Telex and phone calls became more frequent and tried to bring him back down to earth.

"There are certainly people there who can tell us about the doctor. We might learn something about him."

As far as François was concerned, that was still the best reason he could think of for turning a deaf ear to the Parisian contingent, who, in the other world, were begging him to come back.

The two men went first with the photos. Émilie, who had school that day, would join them the next day. Jacques had contacted some of his acquaintances in Miquelon and arranged to set up the exhibition in the community hall.

The night they arrived in Miquelon, François called Émilie.

"There's been a change of plans! We can't put the exhibition up in the community hall. There isn't enough light."

In fact, she remembered that because she had once gone one Sunday afternoon for a dance at cocktail hour—perhaps it had been Bastille Day? The hall had only a few small windows high up on the wall, and they did not give much light to the dance floor or the tables. The smell of warm beer, fiddle music, and the summer heat came back to mind.

"What are we going to do, then?"

"Jacques is going to talk to the priest and see if we can hang the photos in the church. It's that or nowhere."

Because there was no museum in Miquelon, no conference room, no library, there was not much choice: if the community hall did not work, the church would have to do.

"When do you get here?"

"Everything's backwards," she replied with a laugh, not paying attention to what she was saying. "Usually I'm the one who spends my life waiting for you."

There was a brief silence at the end of the line; she could sense that he was smiling.

"Tomorrow, on the mail boat," she answered. "I leave at eight o'clock and will be in Miquelon by mid-morning."

She was not sure how long the crossing would take, because she had never taken the mail boat to Miquelon. For her, boats only went to one place: Langlade.

"Hurry. We don't want to hang the photos without you."

As if I had any control over the time I arrive, she

thought. A childish impatience under the mask of a grown man.

"I'll come and wait for you on the wharf," he added, suddenly touched by the idea that this time it would be him waiting for her.

A few weeks of sharing the satisfaction and excitement of the Doctor Thomas exhibition with her, watching her bloom a little more each day as others came to appreciate her, hearing her muse about the mysterious doctor, construct hypotheses and then describe—with uncommon insight and contagious enthusiasm—the aesthetic value of the photos, had enabled him to define a few of the diffuse emotions that drew them together. Somewhere, in the unfathomable depths of the soul, a world which cannot be expressed in words because it would slide from the sublime into the ordinary, she and he were one. He was hers, she was his.

As for Doctor Thomas, it was the ambiguity of his photos that had allowed them to discover each other.

The crossing from Saint-Pierre to Miquelon was a complete novelty to Émilie. Although she knew every little step between her home and Langlade—first Le Colombier, then the moment right after Henry's Pass where the sea and its currents had a few surprises in store when it was windy, then the rolling waves in the middle of the bay and, finally, every cove, every cliff and every rock on the coast of Langlade—she knew nothing about the trip to Miquelon. The boat sailed on the other side of Le Colombier, where the puffins made their nests. These ocean clowns, with their funny big red beaks, yellow lips and white circles around their eyes as if they were made-up for the circus, hung by the hundreds off the rocky surface.

Leaning on the railing despite the cool autumn morning, Émilie, not so used to sailing that she would stay inside, looked at the Langlade coast from a completely different perspective. First came Anse-aux-Soldats, then the Cap Percé and the Cap aux Morts. She could make out the Gouvernement Cove with its houses that looked like confetti, and marvelled at the fact that the dune did not even appear over the horizon. "No wonder there were so many shipwrecks in the past! In bad weather, you would think you were in the middle of the ocean!" Except for the two big hills, which were given the off-colour name of Mother Dibarboure's Tits (Mrs. Dibarboure was the wife of the farmer in the area at the end of the nineteenth century, according to her grandmother, of course), the waves were hiding the dune.

After about an hour on the open sea, she caught sight of the rocks of Miquelon, minuscule reefs that she had heard about, because you could see, from Langlade, their foam swirling up angrily when the nor'easters announced, without prior warning, that summer was over.

She was discovering the other side of the Langlade scenery, a little as if she had been invited backstage after a performance. Just beyond the rocks of Miquelon, the other side of the hills came into view: Belliveau, the beginning of the Mirande pond, Chapeau, and finally the village of Miquelon, closed off on the right by its imposing cape.

When she got close to the wharf, she started looking for him. There was quite a crowd that morning, people waiting for someone, or for a package, a letter, an order (a can of paint that you could not get on the island, a pair of glasses that had been sent to Saint-Pierre to be fixed, a special gift ordered by phone from the Trouvailles gift shop), people who were curious to see what was going on. In fact, Émilie was one of the curiosities that morning, because people had seen her on television, and besides, François was there waiting for her.

"The priest said yes," he announced right away.

The time was not right for anything more than two kisses on the cheek and a bit of small talk.

"Come on, I'll show you. Jacques is there now. He's waiting for us to tell him how to arrange the photos."

They walked side by side down the road that led directly from the wharf to the church—the very road where Doctor Thomas had set up his camera to take pictures of the people working on the beach—replying to greetings along the way. She could still feel the rocking of the waves in her legs, a strange floating sensation, and she thought it might have more to do with this exceptional life that she had led for the past few weeks than with the movement of the ocean. All of a sudden, she remembered the crushed feeling she had experienced, ten months earlier, as she left the photography studio and realized that she and François could not see each other that afternoon to discover Doctor Thomas. Today, on the other hand, she felt as though she had only to open her arms to fly away.

They found the photographer in the church, deep in conversation with a tiny woman: "Sister Hilarion," whispered François. "You'll love her; she's adorable."

He made polite introductions. The sister, who was called "Mother" by the people of Miquelon as a sign of respect, was indeed very charming. She had a soft voice, but Émilie had the feeling it hid a strong personality. She looked at everyone she met with tenderness, and her behaviour reflected true human compassion. She was discreet enough to bid her farewells shortly after Émilie arrived, to let them get back to their work.

"Here, take the keys, Jacques, and lock the door behind me," she said. "That way no one will disturb you. I know everyone here is eager to see the photos, and you'll see there are plenty who remember the doctor. I don't, unfortunately."

"She was the one who convinced the priest to let us use the church," explained Jacques when she had left. "She told him it was important for the people of Miquelon to remember their past, and for the children to learn about it."

They talked for a while about how to group the photos so that they would make the greatest possible impact on the viewers. They finally agreed to hang them on the elegant light-coloured wooden pillars that supported the building. It was the only place available. Along the walls, under the stained glass windows, an impressive display of the Stations of the Cross took up nearly all the room, and numerous statues occupied what space was left. As the photographer commented, the photos would be displayed in the full light. Once these details were looked after, they got to work. At noon, they walked across the square to eat in the pension where they were staying.

As they ate, they heard the announcement on the radio: "The population of Miquelon is invited to view the photography exhibition *The Islands of Doctor Thomas* from three to five o'clock this afternoon and from nine to ten-thirty this evening at the Notre-Dame-des-Ardilliers Church. The exhibition will also be open to the public tomorrow after Mass until noon. Admission is free."

A few hours after they had eaten, everything was ready. A pure and bright autumn sunlight flowed through the stained glass windows that afternoon, taking on the soft hues of the Biblical scenes and giving the photographs a sepia tone that added to their magical quality.

At three o'clock on the dot, the people of Miquelon, delighted to have been included in the adventure and curious to see these photos they felt belonged to them as well, were lined up at the door.

The exhibition was a great success. A few people found it a little irreverent to use the House of the Lord as an art gallery, but the majority did not mind at all. People crowded around the photos, and the newcomers had trouble getting close enough to admire the details.

Little by little, people relaxed and their voices became a bit louder than the whispers usually heard in the church.

"Surely the priest has put away the Blessed Sacrament," declared a woman who knew the rites and wanted to reassure the faithful.

Just as it was in Saint-Pierre, everyone in Miquelon commented on the photographs. The three of them were silent and attentive, listening for any piece of information they could discover about the doctor who, clearly, had dearly loved Miquelon and its inhabitants.

"I never saw him without a camera in his hand," said an old man who was leaning on his cane and whose knees seemed to give him a lot of pain when he moved. He added, pensively, "That was before the war, of course..."

He pointed to the photograph of the doctor sitting on the capstan with the baby seal in his arms. "I was there," he declared proudly. "It was my father who caught that seal in the Grand Barachois. The doctor had just come back from the war. He didn't stay long on the front; he was injured and sent back to Miquelon. He did his work and everything, but he wasn't the same man. He didn't carry his camera around anymore and he was sad...Like that day. My father wanted to cheer him up a bit." He leaned in again to look at the photo more closely, and then said, "I guess he didn't succeed."

The old man sat down on the bench close by, admiring the photo, entranced by the memory of that fleeting moment of carefree pleasure in a childhood marked by labour and hardship.

Unlike their experience in Saint-Pierre, where they were besieged by friends, relatives, and acquaintances, here in Miquelon no one had much to say to the three people who had organized the exhibition, except to Jacques who had a few old friends dating back to when they were children playing in the fields during the haying or hide-and-seek in the stable or barn at the farm in Pointe au Cheval.

On the other hand, people didn't leave the church. They still congregated around the photos with a quasi-religious admiration. They tried to situate each scene, recognize the people in it, identify the date when it was taken if it was not listed on the labels.

Towards the end of the afternoon, Sister Hilarion arrived with a very stooped old woman on her arm. Judging by her reluctant gait, she had not come here entirely of her own accord but rather because Mother had asked her to. "Nobody in Miquelon ever says no to her," Jacques had explained to them earlier that day.

"Please tell them about it," the nun said gently to the old woman.

"I remember Doctor Thomas," she began. "And his wife and daughter too. They were always together, and he always walked around with his camera in hand. They really loved Miquelon, all three of them. Their daughter was born here. The doctor left for the war, but he came back pretty quickly because he had been wounded. We were all glad he started working here again; he was a fine doctor, a very nice man, not conceited at all. He and his wife did whatever they could to help out poor people. That's why he had problems too."

"Problems!" the three of them exclaimed in unison. "What kind of problems?"

"I'm not too sure, but it had something to do with the beachboys working on the shore. You know, those poor men worked from morning until night drying the fish on the beach. It was really something. They had to lay the cod out on the pebbles, not just any old way but so it would be best exposed to the sun and the wind, and then they had to turn it over after one or two days and make especially sure it wasn't left out in the rain, or even the pissy mist. It had to be picked up quickly and piled up under a tarp when it was wet out, and that was very often, of course. Thankfully people don't have to do that anymore. It was like forced labour, done by boys who were twelve, fourteen years old at the most. The older boys, they were fishing in the dories. And every year, new boys were brought in from France to do that terrible job, and it didn't pay them much either. They must have been really unhappy at home to want to do that job," she concluded.

"But what did the doctor do to get himself into trouble?" Jacques asked.

"I didn't really understand what it was," the lady muttered, "but I think it had something to do with *La Morue française* merchants. I think that's why the doctor went back to France in 1916. For sure, the Thomases wouldn't have gone back on their own without a good reason; they were happy here."

"Yes, fine, but what could he have done, Doctor Thomas, to draw the wrath of *Mémé* and be forced to go back?"

In the Miquelon office of La Morue française, *the cod company from France, the manager angrily pushes his chair back from his desk, stands up, and paces around his office.*

"He wrote what?"

"He wrote that La Morue française *was practising slavery, that in our day it was unacceptable to treat people—children, he said—the way the beachboys are treated. But that's just the beginning of his letter. According to what I heard, he sent a whole medical report to France, with photos and everything."*

The man telling the story is an employee from Saint-Pierre, sent by his bosses to inspect the facilities in Miquelon. What he knows of this business is what he heard a few days before from raised voices coming from the office of the district manager, Mr. Légasse. The reason he is talking about it today is because he knows that Doctor Thomas is good friends with the manager of the Miquelon office. Better let him know, *the man from Saint-Pierre thinks.* Chances are, things are going to get bad!

Once the man has left his office, the manager collapses

into his chair and puts his head in his hands. *Louis had warned him about what he was going to do, but he thought he had persuaded him not to.*

"It won't do any good," he had told the doctor. "The beachboys need the money. And they need a doctor!"

"That's just it! It's my job to denounce this situation," Doctor Thomas retorted. "If not, I'm useless here!"

"But doing so won't get you anywhere either, except to be recalled back to France!" The district manager of La Morue française *knew that the long arm of the Légasse family was capable of anything.*

"I'm sure that's true," the doctor concluded, weary from their long and frustrating discussion. "Let's talk about something else, shall we?"

The manager believed the incident was over, and that his friend, the companion who had taught him everything he knew about photography and who had walked the hills of Miquelon from one end to the other with him, had seen the light. I should have known he wouldn't listen to me, *he thinks. That day, the doctor had shown up at his house in an agitated state. A young beachboy had just died, carried off by a raging fever the doctor had been unable to do anything about. The death had provoked such an angry reaction from the doctor that he had launched into a tirade about forcing such young boys to work, and especially to live, in these horrific conditions.*

The manager of the Mémé, *as the company was nicknamed, knows all about it. He too is concerned about the attitude of the head of the beachboys, a brute hired by Mr. Légasse who seems to take a malicious pleasure in torturing the beachboys under his charge. But that is a special case; they are not all bad and, besides, it is the same everywhere. Every spring, hundreds of young boys rush to be hired as beachboys, ready to agree to anything in order to make a living. The proof is that no sooner had the poor boy been buried than six more were lining up to take his place.*

"Louis may as well pack his bags," his friend sighs.

Five

It was time to pack up the exhibition once again, return to Saint-Pierre, and prepare the photographs for their long trip to France. François made the rounds to say his farewells, and Émilie began mentally preparing herself for their separation. He could tell she was apprehensive about the return to her ordinary life. He realized as well that the wave of creative energy he usually had after a long and restful visit to the islands would take a while to set in this time. It had been weeks since he had thought about his work, his drawings, his projects. But he knew he had to go back. *How long until I can stop complying with these demands?* he began to think for the first time ever. *And why am I doing it anyway?*

To close this particular chapter, Émilie's parents were kind enough to prepare a farewell dinner for the three adventurers. Jacques and his wife and François and his mother sat together at the dinner table. It was as if the Thomas family had joined them as well, that was all they could talk about.

"If the doctor sent a report to his superiors about the conditions of the beachboys and their state of health, the report must be in the Navy's files somewhere," Émilie's father explained.

"But he was a doctor..."

"Yes, of course, but a physician working for the Navy, as they all were in Saint-Pierre et Miquelon at that time. If someone did some research, I'm sure some papers would turn up."

A knowing look exchanged across the table was enough for her to understand that François intended to start looking as soon as he got back to Paris. Retracing the doctor's footsteps, uncovering the traces of his life and work, bringing his secrets into the light of day— François knew it was a link between him and Émilie and a way to extend their exceptional parallel life.

The moment of his departure was upon them. François could not afford the luxury of taking the long road through Newfoundland; he had to get back to France as soon as he could. The Air Saint-Pierre flight would take him to Sydney, Nova Scotia, then on to Montreal in the evening, and early the following morning he would land in Paris. The precious photos would be checked into the baggage compartment. His mother considered the extra expense extravagant, but he was determined.

"The important thing is that they're on this flight with me. I can't stand the idea of being separated from them," he explained to Émilie, "any more than I can stand leaving you."

They were side by side in the small airport. It seemed as if the entire population of the island surrounded them;

in addition to the travellers and their loved ones, there were also curious onlookers who never missed the departures and arrivals, in order to know "what was going on." Just as they used to go down to the wharf to greet the weekly arrival of the mail boat, now they drove to the airport.

Their farewells were restrained. In any case, what could they say that they had not said already? He made no promises to her, nor she to him. Amidst all the activity, they were content to just touch hands briefly, brush elbows, and their eyes never left each other. And then, unable to tolerate the interminable farewell any longer, Émilie said that she had to go. She could not be late for class. She gave him a quick kiss on each cheek and then fled as quickly as she could. He smiled sadly, watching her as she flew off, never looking back.

Twenty minutes later, from her classroom, she could hear the sound of the airplane banking slowly above the town. At that time, she felt doubly abandoned—by François and by Doctor Thomas. Soon the sound faded and once again she felt the unbearable absence, just as before. She felt such a wave of despair that she thought she was going to smother. Her ordinary life had returned.

Daily life resumed, with its routine of classes, homework, walks with friends, hockey games, and hours on the skating rink punctuating the days that seemed to go by in slow motion. Except for a few brief visits to Jacques' studio to fill her heart with their complicity, she found peace only in her writing. She would read over and over again the highlights of the last couple of months and then write down that day's feelings. As she sat in front of the white sheet of paper, watching her pen rush from one line to the next at a dizzying pace, she sometimes found it hard to believe that she had experienced all these intense emotions. She did not feel the same as she did before. It was as if she was preparing to enter the adult world. Amidst the long periods of uncertainty about her future, she also had experienced some calm and serene moments when she was comfortable with her life and seemed to have a more solid footing. On the other hand, she would feel moody, with conflicting emotions, which left her even more troubled than the last time. "What do I want to do with my life?" she wondered.

Nonetheless, she had a pleasant impression that her exceptional parallel life had not vanished completely; instead of his usual silence, of the forced separation which made her so sad between his visits, this time François had kept in contact with her. He wrote her and phoned her regularly.

As soon as he returned to France, he had set off quickly on his search. Between two trips, to Berlin and Tokyo, he had taken off in search of the doctor. A friend who had worked in the Navy museum before retiring suggested he visit the Navy archives in Vincennes. François made many discoveries. Although the doctor may not have left many traces of his life in Saint-Pierre et Miquelon, the public service he worked for had followed his every step.

The first updates took no time to reach Émilie.

"Doctor Thomas couldn't stay still, it seems," she explained to Jacques, reading the first installment of the biographical sketch François was putting together.

After studying at the Navy School of Medicine in Bordeaux and then Toulon, Doctor Thomas was very young when he came to Saint-Pierre et Miquelon in 1912. He left for the war in 1914, returned to the islands in 1916, then went back to France in 1917. He was promoted to the rank of Physician, First-Class. Then there are documents of him getting a vaccine ready for the Navy in 1922. He was back on the islands from July 14, 1923, to May 17, 1926.

"Nearly three years! That's good."

"Like the majority of postings for civil servants," Jacques reminded her.

"You can't say that he was idle during that time."

Appointed Chief of Health for the islands, he sat on the Fisheries advisory committee and various other commissions. He was responsible for a number of health and social assistance initiatives, in particular the elimination of the old institution of beachboys and local campaigns against venereal disease and alcohol abuse during the Prohibition.

"My goodness! First he took on the cause of the beachboys, then smuggling...He was a real trouble-maker, wasn't he?"

Émilie spoke to her grandmother about it.

"During the Prohibition in the United States and Canada, alcohol flowed like water here. Alcohol was imported legally and then taken in speedboats to the coasts of Canada and the United States at night. Whatever happened under the cover of the night and on the open sea were of no concern to the merchants who made millions smuggling it in. Think about it: a merchant made ten cents on every bottle that went through his warehouse, and cases were coming in by the hundreds of thousands. This fraud lasted for over a decade. Imagine all that money!" added Émilie's grandmother emphatically.

Math was not Émilie's strong suit, but a quick

estimate was enough to make her gasp.

The idea that the doctor raised his voice in the middle of this commercial euphoria, to try and control alcoholism and prostitution, must have upset many people.

"Certainly," her grandmother continued, "because before Prohibition, well before Doctor Thomas arrived, the islands went through a very difficult period. Cod was rare, and many people weren't getting enough to eat. That was one more reason for everyone, rich or poor, to be happy when the Americans came in with their fat wallets to buy liquor. They needed men to haul, load, and unload the Cutty Sark, rum, cognac, rye, and scotch; they needed construction workers and carpenters to build the new warehouses to store all the alcohol. There was lots of work for everyone."

"I'm sure the doctor wasn't the only one who complained," suggested Émilie.

"Oh, definitely! The smuggling and bootlegging caused a lot of grief to a lot of people, because liquor cost next to nothing, money was flowing as fast as the alcohol, and hundreds of rather shifty Americans would show up on the shore in the middle of the night, fill up the bars, and then leave again after taking advantage...But in the circumstances, yes, he would have had trouble being heard, I'm sure!"

Émilie went back to the studio to re-examine the photos taken during the Prohibition. She had only reviewed this series quickly when she was getting the exhibition ready, because she found nothing in these photos relevant to François or Doctor Thomas.

As she looked more closely at the photos, she could understand why the series had not inspired her. The photos showing cases of alcohol stacked up and a bee-hive of activity on the wharfs had a heavy atmosphere. The men and their teams of horses—dark silhouettes cut out of a grey autumn or white winter bleakness—seemed to be crushed by the weight of their labour. No smiles, no horses snorting with impatience, nothing light about the movement or colour in these photos. Men and beasts laboured at their tasks, enslaved by this new economic activity, exploited.

She thought again about the photos of fishermen. Fishing was also exhausting labour, but these photos were different. They showed the dignity of men, smiling despite the cold or the pain, standing tall with their heads high. Not like the men in the photos of smuggled liquor, who were hunched over as if held by a yoke that restrained men and animals. The message was clear: There was no honour in that work.

"I'm guessing he didn't drink," concluded Jacques.

A woman trying her best to hide her face leaves the hospital quickly and walks awkwardly by the snow banks along the side of the road before disappearing completely from view. With a heavy sigh, the doctor closes the door behind her and presses his forehead to the glass for a moment.

A broken rib, a dislocated ankle—she must be in such pain! *he thinks, overcome with a bone-numbing exhaustion.*

The woman had been brought to him that morning by a nun who had found her on her way to Mass. She was curled up near a snow bank, her face swollen.

"A few more hours and she would have frozen to death, Doctor!" the nun had cried, horrified. Despite her injuries,

the patient refused to be admitted to the hospital. They had just barely managed to bandage her up before she ran off to get home.

"It's nothing, doctor. My husband isn't bad, you know. But when he drinks..."

Prohibition! Yet again! *The sister, who knows everyone on the island, told him that the woman's husband was one of the numerous fishermen who had found a new career unloading cases of alcohol from the ships that arrive every week from France and transporting them to the warehouses owned by merchants in Saint-Pierre. Then they wait for the Americans to sneak in and load the bottles into their speedboats.*

The doctor is well aware of the situation. He often goes out to the wharves to watch them at work, and even takes photographs. The whole thing seems tremendously sad.

People worked day and night, "especially night," he repeats rather sarcastically, thinking not only of the smuggling but also the restaurants, dance halls, and speakeasys that offer to relieve Americans of their wealth in return for a "French experience."

"In the past, it was the sea that killed these men, or a phlegmon or a case of bronchitis. Now it's money and liquor that poisons them!" he thundered in front of his wife one day.

"Now, now, Louis," said his wife in a soothing tone. "It's not all so bad. Prohibition has given money to people in need. You remember how hard life has been for fishermen the last few years; they lived in misery..."

She was probably right. Still, Doctor Thomas can not help thinking that the islands had, to a certain extent, lost their innocence. They had slid into alcohol and vice, and there is no longer a place for him here.

Émilie studied the Prohibition photos for weeks, examining them with a critical eye. The photos were teaching her, better than any class could, how to use the everyday to express the deepest feelings. And doing so without altering the gestures of the workers or their environment, simply through the composition of the scene and the position of the photographer.

One of the photos stood out from the others. Next to a big boat and the wharf, on which hundreds of cases of alcohol were piled up, were two dories, "coupled up," and across from them a young man leaning on the mooring post. He had a dreamy-eyed expression, was well-dressed, and looked relaxed. Despite this, Émilie imagined that he was looking at the two fishing boats with nostalgia.

"It's as though he is remembering a forgotten era, the dignity of fishermen and their triumph over adversity," she said.

"I hadn't noticed that," Jacques commented, surprised at her interpretation. "There is certainly something interesting to be said on the subject. A course on art appreciation, based on Doctor Thomas' photographs, perhaps?"

"That would definitely put some local flavour into the school curriculum," she added. "That way, we could learn more interesting things about the islands than just the definition found in geography textbooks: 'Islands located in North America, French colony, population 6,000. Harsh climate. Abundant snow in winter, fog in summer. And so on.'"

Some time later, François sent her another installment of Doctor Thomas' biography.

A fervent amateur of dory construction and navigation, Thomas was given an Award of Merit for sailing 3,600 kilometres at the helm of vessels on the seas off Newfoundland, and for his part in designing the first dory with a relatively high-speed motor.

"Is there anything that man didn't do?"

Apparently not:

In 1938, Louis Thomas became Chief Physician, First Class. An assistant to Professor Calmette at the Pasteur Institute, he served on the standing committee for rheumatism of the Ministry of Public Health, and also on the committee on health services for Spanish refugees. He went to the Cantabrian front, where he organized and managed a screening service for contagious diseases, sometimes during bombing episodes and even when he was detained for a while by Franco's forces.

"Another war! Do you think there is a series of photos of the Spanish Civil War somewhere, like the series on the fisheries or the one on the Prohibition?"

"No doubt," replied Jacques, "just like there is probably one on the Great War."

To think they had wondered if he had died shortly after he went back to France or that he had been reduced to a shadow of himself by his struggles! Not only had he continued to move up through the ranks of his profession, but his curiosity had also led him in such fascinating directions.

This portion of the biography of Doctor Thomas elicited, with even more urgency, the mystery question: Why had he left his precious collection of photos on the islands? Why had he not contacted his fellow photography buffs, or his other friends from the islands? Why had Marthe never written to her classmates?

In any case, if the man had burnt the bridge that connected him to the islands, it was not because of anything that incapacitated him—he was still fighting every imaginable battle—but for some other reason. François told Émilie on the phone that he had found out something about Doctor Thomas during the Second World War: "In 1940, he refused to pledge allegiance to the Vichy government, was put on armistice leave, and sent to Algeria. Since he wasn't the kind of man to just take it easy, he returned in secret to Toulon in 1941 and joined the special services of the Resistance. When Paris was liberated, he was with the French interior forces. Then he took part in the liberation of Lorient, both as physician and photographer. Imagine, he recorded the German surrender in his photographs!"

"That's incredible!"

"Wait! I'm not done. At that point, he left for Germany to be a doctor for prisoners of war. He was decorated with the Military Cross and the Legion of Honour. That's pretty special."

"What was his family doing all this time?"

"That's the strange thing. I can't find anything about them at all. There is no mention of them in these archives."

"Does it say what he did after the war?"

"No, but he must have been getting old by that time. I'll keep looking. And I'll put a portrait of the doctor I found in the archives into the mail for you. It dates back to the 1930s. You'll see, it's pretty interesting."

The photograph was a conventional shot and looked like any other official portrait taken in those days. But something about it troubled François. He was not sure why. He counted on Émilie's opinion to help him understand.

She waited for the mail with a bit of trepidation. Aside from the view of the island and the photograph of the doctor on the capstan in Miquelon, she had never seen a close-up or a good full portrait of the doctor.

"When you get the portrait, look at it carefully," Jacques suggested. "A person's expression, hands, forehead, stance…all that can be really telling. They sometimes reveal the true person."

Two weeks later, the eagerly awaited envelope arrived.

She knew the mail boat had landed that day and hurried home after school. Inside the envelope she found a note glued on a second manila envelope: "I would like to introduce you to the man who has been occupying our thoughts for months. I have made a copy of it for my files. Please, let me know as soon as you can what you think of it. The second copy is for Jacques."

She opened it quickly and found herself face to face with Doctor Thomas.

A wave of nostalgia—of genuine sorrow—emerged from the image. The man was sitting and looking to one side, into the lens. His hair neatly combed back, he was well-dressed in a suit, a white shirt, and a tie attached to the collar with a pin, and he had tucked his right hand halfway into his pocket. His left hand rested on his thigh. There was nothing pretentious or affected in his manner. Louis Thomas was posing with good will, but his thoughts seemed to be elsewhere.

Émilie read the sorrow in his empty gaze, in the wrinkles of his high forehead and around his eyes, his unsmiling mouth, the lips hidden under his moustache. All that was painful to see.

"What suffering!" she sighed.

Despite its classic appearance, the photo sent a cry through the years that seemed to pierce her eardrums. She drew her attention away from the doctor's unbearable gaze and studied the hand in the foreground. It was an artist's hand: graceful, strong, lined with wide veins, a hand that conveyed the force and the character of this uncommon man, but also betrayed his unparalleled fatigue. And there should have been a wedding band on this hand, but it was completely bare.

The other one, partially hidden by his jacket pocket, showed something shiny, a bracelet. Or was it a ring?

The emotion she felt became almost intolerable. She set the photograph aside and concentrated on the letter that accompanied it. François explained to her where and how he had found the portrait and added some details to the doctor's biography. A few minutes later, incapable of thinking of anything else, she returned to the portrait.

Louis Thomas' eyes moved her deeply. Why, though? Staring at the image for a long time, she realized that a contradictory feeling was reflected in the man's face, an inner peace mixed with a pain that seemed to have been appeased slightly, but not completely. The man was no longer suffering, it seemed, but he had definitely suffered terribly in the past. What had happened to him? How had this infinite sadness been imprinted on his features, only to finally make room for a certain serenity tinged with resignation?

The secret of Louis Thomas was hidden in this portrait. She placed the photo in full view above her desk and got into the habit of contemplating it for long periods of time. When she opened her diary, it was as if he was staring at her, as if expecting something.

As a writing exercise—she liked grappling with words this way—she tried to write a portrait of the doctor following the instructions on the familiar topic for school compositions: "Describe your favourite character by describing his physical features in a way that reveals his personality." Doctor Thomas did not lend himself easily to this game. He did not meet the usual criteria. His face reflected both pain and joy, in a paradoxical blend that made it useless to try to see where one ended and the other began.

After giving it a lot of thought, she concluded that the photograph did express, on its own, the life experiences of its subject. The sum of his experiences was not made up of its various parts: his tired body, the wrinkles that heavily lined his face. In fact, the opposite was true. In the prime of his life in 1930, Louis Thomas was a handsome man, and he emanated a vital energy. It was in this combination of energy and fatigue that the essence of the man revealed itself: a man who had suffered hard blows, a humanist who was open to the world and who refused to follow conventions, a courageous man whose spirit had not been broken by pain, and despite everything, someone who seemed to look forward to the future, to life.

Émilie, who was so fearful of the future, envied his look that affirmed: "I have lived." The more she looked at it, the more it seemed to want to speak to her. A single question seemed to flow from his lips, full, sensual, and even, she thought from time to time, rather mocking.

"And you, Émilie, what are you going to do with your life? Do you even know?"

For her, it was a question that could no longer be

avoided. In less than a year, her schooling in Saint-Pierre would be finished and she would have her high school diploma. She had no doubt about that part, at least. Even though it was popular for the most serious students to worry about failing, she refused to do so. Of course, some students were jealous of her and would have liked to see her get nervous. These young people called her "arrogant." She had been called that often, but she did not really mind. What did worry her, however, was what she was going to do after she got her diploma, which in the islands bore an odd resemblance to an exit visa.

"What are you going to do later?"

How many times had she heard this question? And she never knew how to answer. The fact that the doctor, too, was now silently asking her from his frame in her room did not surprise her whatsoever. The same question was on the lips of her grandmother, her parents, her girlfriends, and even François. He was, in fact, becoming insistent: "Will you come to France? Promise me you'll come." He wanted her to study in France, in Paris, near him. He dazzled her with what she would be able to study and their proximity which would be such a gift to both of them, and the amazing possibilities that awaited her. She could do anything. He knew it and he did not hesitate to tell her that. Still, she hesitated.

"Why?" he asked her, completely serious. He rarely had doubts about anything, and certainly had none about her.

"I'm not sure what I want to do. It's as simple as that. It isn't a question of what I can do, but what I want to do."

To be honest, she knew exactly what she wanted to do: She wanted to be a writer. The reason she did not tell anyone, that she hardly dared to write it in her diary under the watchful eyes of Doctor Thomas, was that she did not want to commit the horrible sin of pride. It was too hard to say even to Francois—that this was what she wanted to do with her life. Maybe in person she would be able to, but certainly not over the telephone.

Did he sense that she was hiding something? She could feel it every time he called, in every note he scribbled for her on one trip or another. He was determined to convince her come and study in Paris. "Did you apply for university yet?" "Have you decided where you want to study?" He was growing more and more insistent.

"To do what afterwards, though?"

That was the dilemma, for her. As she had read one day in a passage by Jean d'Ormesson, she had a taste for life without being qualified for it. For the time being, at any rate. Given her admiration for Mr. d'Ormesson and his brilliant literary career, this admission by the writer was something of a consolation for her. At least she was not alone in feeling attracted by the world, by writing, and yet totally unconcerned with her future. She realized that this was why she was so fascinated by Doctor Thomas: *He studied medicine, but actually it was something else that nurtured him. He didn't do what was expected of him*, she thought.

And what did people expect of her? She was unable to answer that question. She was intelligent, a gifted student, artistic, and sensitive. She knew she would be able to take on anything and succeed, but she had absolutely no ambition and no career plan. What was she going to do for the rest of her life? How would she channel her energy, her talents? How was she going to make a decision that would not disappoint her parents, and François? How do you go about becoming a writer?

Every time the question came up, she was tempted to reply that the only ambition she had was to be happy and to make the people around her happy. That was the simple truth, because she could not imagine being happy unless she wrote.

As the date of her matriculation exams came closer, she still did not know where she would continue her studies. She knew she had to fill out the application forms and apply for scholarships right away, but she had no interest in doing it. There was no program, no university courses or degree listed for students who wanted to be writers. In no way did she feel capable of asking, as casually as possible, "I'd like to be a writer. What do you think?"

It is easy enough to answer the question "What do you want to do later?" with "doctor," "teacher," "lawyer," "fisher," or even "notary," but she could not see herself saying she wanted to be a writer. "That doesn't sound very serious," some of her teachers would remark, while her classmates would answer, "Arrogant !" No, she had to think of something else and trust her secret to her Clairefontaine notebook.

While she continued to think about her dilemma, the revelations about Doctor Thomas' activities continued to make their way across the ocean, reinforcing her initial impressions she got from his gaze.

In June 1948, he defended his doctoral thesis in Natural Science in Paris: "A contribution to the comparative histopathology of fish."...He was the assistant director of the cancer research laboratory at the École des hautes études.

"Along with all the rest, he had a doctorate in science! He must have loved studying!"

The little bits and pieces of Doctor Thomas' biography always arrived with a note or a little anecdote from François. He had not been back to Saint-Pierre since the exhibition, but he was very present in her life. He phoned to tell her how his clients had reacted in such or such a way to the photos that filled his office.

"Saint-Pierre et Miquelon? I thought it was warm there. It's in the French Antilles, isn't it?"

Or else: "What are they doing, those people on the frozen pond?"

"They're sawing the ice, Madam."

Émilie laughed, amused by the fact that the photos were doing their job and happy to be taking part, through Doctor Thomas' photographs, in his everyday life. And every time, he asked what she was planning to do in the fall.

"I'm not sure," she replied, disappointed that she could not even confide in him, the one person to whom she thought she could tell everything.

"...Not sure, that's a bit vague."

She wished she could toss out as a matter-of-fact, "Writer. I've decided to be a writer." How would he respond to that? She had no idea. Despite everything that connected them, she was afraid. Not so much of his reaction, as what it would mean to state out loud the enormity of her ambition.

One Saturday morning François called her, very excited. At first she thought he must be calling because he had uncovered the thirty final years of Doctor Thomas' life.

This was the period that was shrouded in mystery. In the 1950s, when he was in his sixties, he had slowed down his medical practice. Perhaps he had retired. But what did he do? Where did he go?

But that was not it. His enthusiasm hinged on something else. After months of negotiations, which he had not mentioned to her because he was afraid she would be disappointed if it had not worked out, the Marine museum and the Department of Overseas Territories had agreed to co-host an exhibition entitled *Louis Thomas, an Exceptional Doctor.*

"It is a bit like a sequel to our exhibition in Saint-Pierre. I was waiting to be sure it would happen to talk to you about it, but I've been working on it for a while now."

She was speechless.

"I'll let you guess how much energy I've put into this, and how many contacts I've used to convince everybody. I had to stroke them a bit," he admitted, laughing. He had mentioned that Doctor Thomas had been an honour to France in the colonies, and they could verify that in their archives. The curator of the museum could not get over it.

"He was a student of the famous Professor Calmette, he led a mission to the Grand Banks, and he published an exhaustive study of the dory, just to mention a few things! And nobody knows about him!"

The two departments were also on Doctor Thomas' trail. But they needed the glass plates, which were essential for the production of the exhibition.

"Émilie, we're putting you in charge of bringing them to France. The museum will pay your fare. Jacques agreed to let us have them, but it is out of the question for us to send them in the mail."

"Why me?"

"Jacques can't close the studio so close to Easter. But he will come over for the opening. The museum will also pay for his trip."

So it was as simple as that. *When you've built houses all over the world, your perspective isn't the same,* she thought affectionately. Even in her wildest dreams, she would not have been able to imagine such an adventure.

A few weeks later, during the Easter holidays, she left for Paris for the first time in her life. Her mission was to escort Doctor Thomas' photographs back to his homeland.

François had won. Dismissing all of the objections, finding solutions to every problem, he had looked after everything: airline tickets, lodging—the museum was paying for everything. After just a few phone calls, everything was in place. He talked to her parents several times to reassure them. They told him about their own concerns.

"Maybe you can convince her to study in France. She hasn't made a decision yet. It's as though she doesn't want to do anything. And she never talks to us about it."

He promised to take her on a tour of Paris, to visit the Sorbonne, to show her all the incredible charms of the capital. He could already picture her in Saint-Germain-des-Prés, imagine her marvelling over all the little bookshops—she was always looking for something to read—her reverence as she visited the tombs of Voltaire and Rousseau in the Pantheon. He even planned to take her to the cemetery in Montparnasse, where she could kneel down in front of Baudelaire's tombstone, her favourite poet, as she had confided to him one evening when she opened her schoolbag and he found a worn-out copy of *Fleurs du mal.*

It was not the first time someone from Saint-Pierre et Miquelon came to visit him. François often received guests from the islands in Paris: his brothers, or simple acquaintances who came to see the country or, more often, for medical care. François always knew whose door to knock on, how to get an appointment with a famous specialist who was too busy to bother with everyday mortals. He knew all the right places to go and did not hesitate to use his connections. He was a "doer of favours," as his compatriots called him. They appreciated this quality all the more because they knew how well-known he was and how busy. These sporadic visits distracted him for a little while, until some innocent comment from his visitor suggested that they took him for someone else, or they believed him to be deliriously happy when he was not really. Then a "wall" would fall between them, the way the Planck wall is thought by scientists to be the point at which scientific knowledge ends. Nothing that occurs beyond this point makes any sense.

There was no question about it...he was waiting for Émilie with great impatience. She would not be intimidated by the people around him, by this absurd status he had been given. He had learned to adjust to it and did not mind using it to help other people out, especially people visiting him from the islands. On the other hand, he did not take his Parisian life too seriously. Émilie would not either, he was sure of it. Paris would impress her in other ways though. He was already delighted at the thought of what he was going to show her.

When the plane took off from Saint-Pierre, Émilie felt the relief everyone from the islands feels when they manage to get away, which is quite a feat given the weather or the possible mechanical problems. Leaving meant conquering an isolation that people pretended to appreciate ("Here, at least, we don't have to worry about being attacked or assaulted") but which occasionally became stifling.

Being so far off the ground gave her a rare moment of pure meditation. Alone, suspended in the heavens, with nothing to tie her to her familiar world, with no one to make conversation with, she could not escape a moment of self-evaluation.

This trip, which had not even been planned two weeks earlier, would give her a preview of her future, to see "if France and the university there could possibly suit me." She did not have any great illusions about it; since she loved wide-open spaces, the ocean, and the barrens, she could not really picture herself in a big city. She had never been to France, but she had visited Montreal and Toronto and did not have very good memories of them.

What had bothered her about urban life was not so much the noise, the pollution, the crowds, or a certain fear of being attacked, robbed, or constantly jostled in the streets; it was the misery that affected her the most. In Montreal, for example, the drunken man she saw on the street corner ("*robineux*" as they are called), the young people her age with a dazed look who were pan-handling at the entrance of the metro station, the people living in the dingy streets sharply contrasted with the opulent hotels like the Queen Elizabeth or the

Ritz-Carlton or the fancy stores like Holt Renfrew, where her grandmother bought a beautiful fur coat every ten years. All this ugliness, this poverty, barely hidden at the core of all that wealth and glitter. It was painful to see. The city was, in her eyes, the very expression of human distress, a witness to the collective madness of the human race and its frenetic course towards nothingness.

Was it better to confront the misery—to smile at the beggar and give him a dollar—or pretend not to notice and take advantage of the pleasures of the city, its department stores and fine restaurants that were so sorely lacking on the islands? By putting her face-to-face with her urge to buy pretty things and enjoy their distractions, big cities made Émilie uncomfortable. She never quite knew what to do, and felt confused and ashamed of herself. If Montreal and Toronto had this effect on her, she could only imagine that it would be worse in Paris.

France would not suit her, she told herself. François could call her "my little European" all he wanted, and boast of the advantages of Paris, but nevertheless she felt North American, more attracted by wide-open spaces than by a Europe whose population statistics alone made her dizzy. She also suspected that François was not telling her the whole truth. She knew that his success in the country of their Breton, Norman, and Basque ancestors (as they said) had not been enough to make him happy. If he really felt fulfilled, would he come home to the islands so often? Would he not already be married, have a family, be "settled," as they said in Saint-Pierre et Miquelon? She had gathered that he was eager for her to move to Paris in order to fill an important void in his life. And, even though she loved him, she had decided not to do anything that would get in the way of her own quest for happiness.

Accustomed to the serenity of open spaces, the sea, and the distant coasts that one could see in the distance without feeling a need to visit, it was difficult to imagine herself living in Paris. However, that was where her studies would take her, to the Sorbonne, no doubt. But what would she study? Literature? She felt that such legendary institutions would be elitist and conflict with her personality. Competitive exams and friends in the right places, that turned her stomach. She did not want her studies to become a mental military service that made her think only of achievement and success, even at the expense of other students. What was wrong with studying for the pleasure of learning and finding her own way gradually? Were there programs that did not lead directly into specific careers? Why could she not simply study in order to enrich her knowledge, or develop as a person? What could she do while waiting to fulfill her dream of being a writer?

She envied people who had always known what they wanted to do: François, who had always wanted to be an architect, had designed houses when he was fifteen; the orthopedic surgeon who marvelled at the thought that he had never had to think about what he wanted to do, and had pretended to operate on his brother's leg on the kitchen table when he was ten years old. People who decided not to go to university fascinated her just as much: the big bruisers who explained shyly that they had always wanted to live by the ocean, the carpenters who were also shipbuilders, the captains on ocean-going ships or those who owned their own small boats, masters of onshore boats or fishers...all these people who never wondered what they would do with their lives. They had always known. She would have given a great deal to be like them.

However, she did not want a career anyway. The idea of training for a trade or a job and to spend her whole life doing it seemed like a jail sentence. What happened if, ten years later, she got tired of it? For her, it was impossible to envisage a life without change, repeating the same gestures, the same actions. Was it even possible to hope for something more?

"I could stay in Saint-Pierre."

"No!" exclaimed everyone in her family.

The daughter and granddaughter of schoolteachers, she was expected to do more than work as a clerk or a saleslady. Sometimes she would rebel and declare: "It's nothing to be ashamed of!"

"Of course not," her mother replied, "but you have so many options!"

Her family wanted her to "go away to university" because she had the opportunity to do it. Her intellectual abilities had opened up the door and the State now gave young people the means to afford it. Émilie would no doubt get scholarships, and her parents were sufficiently comfortable to be able to pay for however long she wanted to study. Choosing to stay here and get a job right away was a way of ignoring all the sacrifices made by generations who had worked hard and saved in order to make sure their children would have an easier life. She would be an ungrateful heir to those who had studied for years without any help.

"François received a state scholarship," her mother explained. "Ask him to tell you about it. It had a fancy title, but that was about it. They paid a return trip for him every two years and gave him barely enough to live on while he was studying in Europe. Sometimes, he told us, all he had to eat for two or three days was a baguette and a piece of cheese. You'll have enough to live comfortably and come home every year. If you add in whatever we'll give you, you'll be fine."

Émilie had to admit that the idea of staying in Saint-Pierre et Miquelon was as unpleasant as the thought of going away. Her studies had given her a view of the world and developed in her an intellectual curiosity that the islands could no longer satisfy. The books she read had made her an explorer, and her youth gave her a taste for adventure. She wanted to see other things, experience life differently...*But I don't really want to leave, either!* she thought. Her ambivalence was only getting deeper.

Even before she got her high school diploma, she could feel that the islands, their population, and their institutions had joined forces to send her away, to force her to go and see what was happening in other places.

"Nothing you do will keep you from coming back," they added, trying to convince her.

She had her doubts.

She was in this uneasy state of mind when they flew over the coast of France. From the window, she looked at the gentle curves of the coastlines of Brittany and Normandy—she had no landmarks to distinguish them—the irregular patchwork of farms, fields, and forests, the little brick-coloured villages, the houses tight against each other in order to leave a little room for farmlands. Suddenly she felt a lump in her throat; tears blurred her vision, as a song by Jean Ferrat called *Ma France* came back to her. She had heard it years ago and thought she had forgotten it. Why, when she considered herself so North American? When she laughed at François for calling her "my European girl"?

Her convictions shaken, taken aback, this young North American who had claimed the only thing European about her was her ancestry now had her nose glued to the window so she would not miss a single piece of the gradually approaching landscape. The view reminded her of the aerial photos she had pored over in her geography textbooks. It was completely different from Saint-Pierre and Canada. Here, there was no snow anywhere; everything was green. She could even identify the trees in bloom: apple trees, cherry trees, and, as they got closer, vegetable and flower gardens.

And now Paris. The Eiffel Tower, first of all, the winding curves of the Seine, Notre-Dame. She tried in vain to situate herself: the left bank, the right bank, she could not figure it out. She wondered where François' office was. In the end, the only thing that mattered on this expedition was that two men were waiting for her—François and Doctor Thomas—whose portrait she had slipped into her diary and whose face she had stared at many times as they flew over the Atlantic. She was still trying to figure out the circumstances that led this man to return to France, and why he had never tried to reconnect with the islands.

François was at the airport, looking proud of himself and as impatient as a child at the idea of showing her around his world.

"There you are!"

He rushed to meet her, the way she had done that

winter morning in front of the Pointe aux Canons, the day they had made the acquaintance of Doctor Thomas.

Once he was at her side, he realized that there was something wrong, a sadness perhaps, weighing her down. He looked at her without a word, took her hand, and went over to pick up her suitcase. She could feel in this contact with him an energy that swept away all her indecision.

"So, here's my plan," he announced. "First, we'll bring the plates to my office for safe keeping. Then we'll get you settled at the hotel. Tomorrow morning, first thing, we'll take the plates to the museum and meet the curator. I've invited him to have lunch with us. After that, you can decide what we'll do with the rest of the day. What do you think?"

He had chosen a hotel near his apartment, near the Seine, "on the right bank," he said. Through the car windows, as they moved around the boulevards of Paris, she had the feeling she was travelling through a history book: the galleries of the Louvre stretching along, with its breath-taking architectural precision, the Tuileries garden on the other side of the Seine, the Orsay train station that they were converting into a museum.

"It's so much bigger than I imagined..."

Farther along she glimpsed the menacing towers of the Conciergerie and the steeple of the Sainte-Chapelle. François named all of these places she had heard about in school—*I should have paid more attention*, she thought— and she realized that Paris was not like other cities, certainly not like the young cities of North America. Here, from Notre-Dame to the Lutèce arenas, daily life took place in the middle of French history. The polluted air of the capital did not seem quite as unbearable anymore, and she could even ignore the dark-brown waters of the Seine.

After dropping her bags off at the hotel, he took her to a sidewalk café at Place Colette; "Just a few steps away from the Comédie-Française!" he exclaimed, as he pointed out the famous theatre. She had seen a performance on its stage on television once or twice, but had never even thought about what the building looked like or where it was.

He smiled at her enthusiasm.

"Inside, they even have Molière's armchair. I think you can go in and see it, but I'm not sure."

He got up quickly, spotting a bookstore on the other side of the square, and asked her to wait for a minute.

"You'll need tourist guides and a map so that you can explore the city. I'll be right back." She smiled as she watched him walk away. He was almost skipping like a kid.

"Here are some things to look at tonight, if you don't fall asleep right away," he said a few minutes later, placing his loot on the tiny round table. "Try to find out if we can tour the theatre. We'll find time to go at some point. I am at your service...and that of the doctor."

She smiled happily. It felt like everything was possible now.

To the great frustration of his colleagues, François had tossed the planning for the week out the window. Moreover, he took a mischievous pleasure in doing so.

"How about going for a walk? My legs feel numb

from the airplane," she suggested.

He pushed back his chair and took her arm. They crossed the square, went down the Rue de Rivoli, where the traffic was incredibly busy and loud, then through the grounds of the Louvre to the banks of the Seine. Night was falling peacefully, the trees were adorned with bright new leaves, and there was a gentle spring warmth in the air that would not be felt in Saint-Pierre et Miquelon for two or three months yet.

"It's as warm as it is in the middle of the summer in Saint-Pierre, and there is so much green!"

"That's right," he said, smiling at her surprise, "But smell the air...it's not quite the same here, is it?"

True enough, despite the gentle caresses of spring, the flowers blooming in flower-boxes on balconies, and the bright green leaves newly deployed, there was a lingering odour of exhaust fumes, hot rubber from tires, stagnant water and refuse. Even in the relative calm on the banks, you could hear the noises of traffic, horns, and sirens in the background.

"Listen. It sounds like the ocean on the west shore the day after a storm..."

He burst out laughing, amused at the parallel that seemed so odd but was absolutely correct. *From now on*, he thought, *that's what I'll think about before I start complaining.*

"Can you see, now, why I love the wind and the storm in Saint-Pierre? The air is so clean and fresh, it cleans out my lungs."

She smiled, moved a little closer to him, and adjusted her pace to walk at the same rhythm as he did. She began to think that here, in Paris, in the middle of the pollution and the millions of people around them, they were alone in the world; while on their islands, where there were only six thousand people, in the wilds of nature, they were never alone.

At about the same time, he stopped to look at her, enthralled to see her in this Paris evening, in the place where, decades ago, he had become resigned to solitude.

"Paris is beautiful with you here!"

The curator of the Marine museum, a rear admiral with a rather intimidating physique but debonair, met them in his office the next morning. Émilie was given a quick tour of the public galleries. Then the three of them went into the workshops and offices where, among other things, the Doctor Thomas exhibition was being assembled.

"Here," the curator said, with a sweeping gesture, "are the photos taken during the First World War. The army has loaned them to us. We've made most of the prints. Sit down; I want to show you something amazing."

The curator and his guests took their seats around a large desk, where two beige file folders were set before them. In the first was a photo that dated back to the beginning of the war. It showed a group of soldiers at the front, sitting on a mound of earth eating their lunch—a few carefree minutes in the middle of long days for these men destined to suffer under machine-gun fire. There were little details that emphasized how precarious the moment was: their weapons within arm's reach, their soiled uniforms and muddy boots, the tiny rations they were eating. The soldiers' attitudes reflected the full range of human emotion. One had a lofty pose of a young man confident he could make short work of the German army. Another expressed the inescapable anxiety of someone who feared the worst. The third one had a blank stare, as if he no longer expected anything of the time he had left to live.

Émilie could feel her heart sinking. She turned to François, who nodded his head, sharing her sentiment. In this innocuous setting, and despite the rather pleasant scene of men taking a break to eat together, the photograph conveyed war, drama, sweat, dirt and sulfur.

"Once again, the doctor has managed to express the worst of life through an ordinary event." She sighed.

"Exactly," agreed the curator. "That's what makes his work so interesting. Now, look at this one," he said, opening the second folder.

They were speechless. The second photo had been taken at the same place. The lens had not moved an inch, and the shot was framed the same way. But where an instant before three soldiers had been eating their ration, now there were only twisted bodies, torn apart like the mound of earth behind which they had taken shelter.

"It looks as though the doctor was protected from the explosion because he was standing a few steps out of the way, taking the picture," he commented. "That may be when he got his injury. We're trying to confirm the facts."

"How could he have survived such an event?" Émilie asked, her eyes glued to the carnage.

"A stroke of luck," replied the curator.

"Remember, in Miquelon, people told us he came back from the war and he wasn't the same person," François said, guessing that she was not trying to figure out how the doctor had escaped the blast, but rather how he had managed to go on living.

"As you can guess, those two photos will be part of the exhibition," the curator stated. "They are absolutely unique. We're still looking for the ones he took during the Spanish Civil War."

"After this, I wonder where he found the courage to pick up his camera and go to help the Republican troops in Spain," François said.

"Especially since he didn't have to go, the way he did in 1914," she added.

"The more closely we examine his career, the more obvious it becomes that Doctor Thomas was only happy when he was in the centre of the action," the curator continued. "He seemed to have volunteered for every task, complex or petty, as long as there was something new to see and learn. They don't make men like that anymore."

Once more she looked at both photos side by side. For anyone, like her, who had not known the horrors of war, the two photos made the soldiers' terror tangible, as well as the ordinary aspect of war. Despite the fear, the thought of death stalking them, the men had to meet their most basic needs: eat, rest a little, maybe even laugh. This was clear in the first photo, in the rather relaxed posture of the soldiers in a kind of cease-fire. Then came the second photo, which made it clear that war did not give anyone a break, that the cease-fire was an illusion, that death could strike at any moment.

The explosion of this rogue shell must have devastated the doctor. She could almost hear, trapped under the jagged rocks, the dying men scream in agony, moan in pain, their limbs ripped apart and their cries lost in the whistling of bullets and the deafening thunder of bombs.

Émilie had to shake that terrible feeling. The curator had other things to show them, photos taken on the Grand Banks during a fishing expedition.

"I've already seen some of these," she explained. "He left a whole series of them in Saint-Pierre."

"The doctor must have printed some of the photos and kept some of the glass plates for himself. They date back to his last stay on your islands, in any case," the curator explained. "When we asked the Navy authorities for Thomas' photos of the French fishing fleet in Newfoundland, they just stared at us...No one knew about the collection. It took a long time to find it."

Since she had seen the war photos taken by the doctor, Émilie had a better understanding of how he had managed to infuse such dignity in the eyes of the exhausted, soiled, and shaggy-haired fishermen.

"Between his atrocious war memories and the feverish commercial activity around the Prohibition in Saint-Pierre, those men must have seemed irreproachable."

"In any case," François agreed, "I have a better idea of why he volunteered for a mission to the banks. I'm sure he appreciated the peace on the sea!"

Now it was time to tell the curator about the series of photos the doctor had taken about the Prohibition, smuggling as it was called in Saint-Pierre et Miquelon. "That's something else to research," François announced.

Flabbergasted by the images she had just seen—by the tragedy that had shaken the doctor's life—Émilie decided to go for a walk. She needed some fresh air, some exercise, and time to reflect before putting the pieces together.

With Émilie on his arm, François took her to the banks of the Seine. They walked silently, comforted by the closeness of their bodies and the harmony of their thoughts.

All of a sudden, Émilie stopped. "The photo of the doctor on the capstan...that's why he looked so sad."

"What do you mean?"

"You know how a seal's noises sound like a child crying? They sound so sad. The doctor had just come back from the war when that photo was taken. He must have felt terrible, hearing the seal's moans. It must have brought back such cruel memories. And the poor fisherman, he was just trying to cheer him up..."

"You're probably right," François said.

He had often thought about that photo, the haggard look in the doctor's eyes. He had assumed it was exhaustion or the fact that the cruel fishers had killed the mother seal and used the babies as circus animals. Now he could see deeper into the doctor's thoughts and knew it was despair in the face of existence and humanity.

They arrived at the Alexandre-III bridge. To lighten the atmosphere a little, François described the architecture of the bridge and pointed out the cherubs playing ivory horns and trumpets.

She smiled sadly. How could people glorify conquest, war, power, when they were all won at the cost of so much blood and grime? Standing before the statues erected to the glory of despots, she suddenly felt as if all the misery of the world had fallen on her shoulders. She was both the vessel and the prisoner of so much suffering: that of Doctor Thomas, with his body and his soul crushed by the war, the three soldiers in the trenches, and all the other nameless victims.

She staggered a bit, steadied herself on the stones of the bridge, and stared at the murky waters of the Seine. She tried to get back to this reality that was so foreign to her; the boundary between real and imaginary was still fuzzy.

Instinctively, François drew her to him in a protective gesture. In his arms, the pain she had felt evaporated as quickly as it had appeared.

"Sometimes," she explained in a whisper, "I feel like I'm drowning."

That was the only explanation she could find for the impression she had never been able to share with anyone.

He held her closer to him, asking nothing more of her. "I found those photos very moving, too. Now I understand why Doctor Thomas was never the same after the war. But I still don't quite understand why he left Saint-Pierre and everything behind."

The reminder of their common mission enabled Émilie to regain her composure. They headed to his office. The receptionist, relieved to see her boss, told him that someone was waiting for him in the boardroom.

"Probably the student I put in charge of research during your visit. I told her to come and meet us."

François took Émilie into his office, where she hung up her coat and put her purse away. She had a chance to look at the photos for a moment. He had placed the photo of the doctor on the island across from his desk and the one on the capstan to his right. She could almost smell the sea air. Then he showed her into the board room to meet the young woman, who seemed extremely excited.

"I just had a really interesting call from the curator at

the Musée national des Arts et Traditions Populaires. They have a collection of about thirty thousand photos by a Louis Le Thomas, a Breton doctor from Landerneau. We think it's the same person, and that he went back to his Breton name at some point."

"What are the photos of?"

"It's fascinating," the researcher continued. "He seemed to have done a complete inventory of Breton religious statuary, village pardons, crosses, wood, stone—everything is there it seems. It had never been photographed before and no one has ever tried to do it since. I checked out the dates and information, and it is definitely your man."

"Thirty thousand photos! That's huge!"

"Yes, taken between 1935 and 1960. That's twenty-five years' work."

"But...is this all the man did after he retired, or was there something else?" asked François.

Émilie smiled. It was just like him to dismiss thirty thousand photos so quickly. Their eyes met and he smiled back at her, happy that she understood him so well.

"Well, the research is coming along," the student replied. "We know that in 1968, Louis Thomas moved into a retirement home in Brittany, in la Baule-les-Pins to be precise. He was 81 years old then. We're still looking for more details, but it's complicated, you know. Once he left the Navy after the Second World War, there isn't any archival material to help us. He was about sixty years old, let's say, and from that time on, besides the Breton statuary, he probably didn't start any other projects."

"Well, 1968 is like yesterday," exclaimed François. "We should be able to track down a Louis Thomas or Le Thomas in Baule-les-Pins. And what about his family?

His wife and daughter? They're in the photos taken in Langlade and Miquelon."

"We found no mention of them anywhere."

Retirement homes, nursing homes, hospices, they made a list of all the places in the area where the doctor might have lived in the last years of his life. The young researcher returned to her search for Louis Thomas, a man who was so attached to his Breton roots that he had decided, as an old man, to call himself Le Thomas again.

"It's a little childish, don't you think, to believe that a name can change the course of a man's life or influence his future!" she said to him.

"Maybe he just wanted to affirm his sense of belonging. After all, he'd lived in a lot of different places: Bordeaux while he was studying, Toulon, then Saint-Pierre et Miquelon, back to France, then Spain, Algeria during the war. Maybe that's why he wanted to spend the last years of his life in Brittany."

"And to put the "Le" back in his name."

While they were talking, they walked calmly up Montagne Sainte-Geneviève Street in the direction of the Pantheon. He was the one who had chosen their destination. He wanted to show her "the building that was supposed to be a church, but that Napoleon had decided otherwise." He hoped that visiting the crypt that housed the tombs of Voltaire, Zola, and Victor Hugo would impress her, and that these great names would give her the inspiration to move forward herself, to leave her own mark on the world.

Their footsteps echoed on the marble floor. The walls of the building rose up to a high ceiling, their white expanses interrupted here and there with murals dedicated to Sainte Geneviève.

"I think I know why the doctor was interested in Breton religious statues," she said suddenly. "I was just thinking about it, as I was looking at all this." She made a grand sweep of her hand. "You don't find the God of the poor and the afflicted in places like this. You can see Him on a little granite cross at a bend in the road, in the little statues painted by local craftsmen, or in the little black saint in the church in Quimper—what's he called, again? I read an article about it. Oh, I know. The *Santik Du*. Churches, cathedrals, they're for kings, the rich... Calvaries are for the people."

He smiled affectionately at her lyrical rendition. "You know what I mean. That collection is just like the rest of his work. He always took the side of ordinary people."

He stared at her with amazement. Why had he not thought of that? Perhaps because he saw Louis Thomas as a man of action more than anything else, a man in the field, a doctor who healed the body rather than the soul, a realist, and no doubt a fervent champion of public schooling, of a free and mandatory education system, like all the other educated and free minds of his time. He had trouble imagining that he was a fervent practising religious man. But a person of faith, yes, no doubt.

They went down into the crypt. Unlike the rest of the building, it was simple, unornamented, a contemplative space where some of the great men of the nation rested in the peaceful torchlight.

"If Paris is a history book, here it is probably *Lagarde et Michard*," she whispered. He wrinkled his forehead. "*Lagarde et Michard*, the literature textbooks we use in high school," she explained.

He smiled, realizing that the visit would not have quite the effect he expected. After all, Voltaire, Rousseau, and Diderot had been buried in simple tombs. And, as she added, "Why is Baudelaire still in the Montparnasse cemetery, instead of here?"

"Good, we'll go see Baudelaire! Then we'll go out to a restaurant and I'll take you back to the hotel."

The next morning he took her out for breakfast at a sidewalk café on the Boulevard Saint-Germain. Then he left her while he went to a business meeting, one of the obligations he had not managed to cancel or delegate to a colleague.

"Go for a little walk and I'll meet you here at noon. After lunch, we'll go to the Musée des Arts et Métiers. We're expected there this afternoon."

She watched him walk off with his determined stride, relieved that she would see him again in a few hours. She made the most of her time alone by sitting and observing everything around her. On the other side of the boulevard were the gardens of the former Hôtel de Cluny. Inside, she had discovered in one of the tourist guides he had bought for her, was the tapestry of the Dame à la Licorne, which, she recalled with amusement, also decorated the cover of another *Lagarde et Michard*, the one on Ronsard, Joachim du Bellay and company. *Two other fellows who do not have a place in the Pantheon.*

She was not tempted to go in, and the Louvre did not really interest her either. She much preferred the people who filled the sidewalks, to watch their expressions and try to inscribe a life story on their features, to give them a family and an occupation. Despite any apprehensions she had, there was a great sense of freedom in the fact that she was here, a stranger in the middle of the crowd, freed of the need to recognize or greet anyone.

She finished her coffee—he had graciously paid the

bill before he left—and started back up the Boulevard Saint-Michel, with no particular destination in mind. When she reached the Rue des Écoles, she turned left. La Sorbonne, the Collège de France, and the Lycée Louis-Legrand were all within a few blocks of her. From Saint-Pierre, she had imagined these prestigious institutions filled with exceptional students, bookworms who spent all their time in dusty libraries, their faces pale from spending all their days in classrooms and study halls. Though judging by the people she saw around her, the schools were full of students who were quite ordinary. Girls her own age, dressed the way she was, with carefree expressions, walked around the neighbourhood. Crocheted bags *stuffed with books*, she thought, hung from their shoulders. Easter break was about to begin, and the students from the Lycée could already taste freedom.

Would there be a place for her in these schools if she had been born in Paris? Was it good luck to have had the best teachers available? The widest range of courses? The numerous museums, libraries, and cultural centres in Paris to complement her studies? Was she at a disadvantage to have grown up in Saint-Pierre? Would her dream of becoming a writer have seemed more plausible, more realistic, if she had gone to a Lycée in this Latin Quarter? At the very least, would the outstanding education acquired here have inspired in her more ambition?

She suddenly envied all the young girls she could hear talking about clothes, music, and boyfriends, as though they could care less about studying at the best Lycée in France. She thought of the high school in Saint-Pierre, which did not even have a library, of the teachers who, every autumn, arrived fresh out of Teacher's College and who were sometimes so incompetent that people suspected they were sent overseas, like the doctors, to cut their teeth before they were allowed to teach in France.

And what did she know about culture? She had never even seen the inside of a theatre, nothing other than Mr. Haran's movie theatre. Of course she had read Molière, Racine, and Corneille, and seen Feydeau on television, but she had never sat in a theatre. And to think I didn't even know where the Comédie-Française was!

Her jealousy mingled with a feeling that she detested equally: shame. She became convinced that she had deluded herself to believe that she could ever become a writer. How could she have made such a mistake? How could she aspire to rise to such heights when she came from so far away?

She stood motionless on the sidewalk (as were the thoughts in her head) and a couple of people bumped into her before she realized she should step back from the crowd.

For months and months I have been fooling myself, she thought, horrified.

She had, of course, been reluctant to make plans, to envisage her future life, but it was not because of a lack of ambition, as she had assumed, but rather because she was afraid. Her fear of the unknown, of not being good enough to do what she dreamed of doing with her life. And the moment this truth revealed itself, another one came to join it: she was deluded to believe in this grandiose dream of becoming a writer.

She turned and walked right back down the boulevard, sat down at the same café, ordered an Orangina, and took her Clairefontaine notebook out of her bag to try to put her thoughts in order. Forgetting the unrelenting noise of horns and odours of exhaust fumes, she tried to untangle this new reality, ignoring the fact that, in this moment of doubt, she had turned to writing the way a drowning man grabs a buoy.

François looked at her from afar. She was completely immersed, chewing on the already misshapen end of her pen. He was surprised that she did not even see him coming. He never failed to notice her worried look when she was waiting for him, then the spontaneous smile she offered the instant she saw him, and every time, it went straight to his heart. In the fleeting instant of recognition, a feeling of serenity came over him. What was going on today, behind her furrowed brow and uncertain eyes, that kept her from greeting the precious happiness they shared?

He came close, and she still did not notice. He placed his hand on her shoulder and it was only then that she became aware of him. She looked at him with an expression of such utter sorrow that he collapsed into the chair across from her.

"What's wrong?" he asked in a worried tone. "Did someone bother you?"

"No, nothing like that. Don't worry."

"Don't worry? Come now, what's going on?"

Where should she begin? How could she explain to him that her life's dream was just an illusion? I have to tell him something, she thought, as she saw François becoming increasingly worried.

She told him about her walk, and the way it disturbed her to see the students who had been so fortunate coming out of the Lycée. "I know they aren't having trouble figuring out what they want to do after they get their diploma."

He could not help smiling a little. He was relieved,

despite feeling Émilie's vulnerability. So the self-reflection he was expecting to provoke by taking her to the Pantheon had occurred in front of a Lycée.

"You too know what you want to do."

"I don't, and you know it! I tell you the same thing every time you ask me, that I have no idea!"

"I know what you tell me," he said gently, "but I also know that it isn't the truth."

Her jaw dropped.

"A girl as intelligent, as sensitive as you are, who knows how to interpret photos, thoughts, the expressions of a man like Doctor Thomas...Come on, you can't tell me that you don't have enough imagination to dream of your future!"

He put his hand on her shoulder, at the base of her neck, where the heart beats so quickly in moments of great emotion, and he held her tightly in order to give her courage. Then he waited.

"Even if I have an idea, I realized this morning that I was dreaming in technicolour. How do you expect me to measure up to these students who have had every advantage to learn, to discover things? Until this week, I didn't even know what a theatre looked like, a real museum, or la Sorbonne," she added, with growing bitterness.

"Really, none of that matters! If it did, every genius in France would've been born in Paris and studied in the Latin Quarter! How do you think I got ahead? By telling myself that because I had only seen frame houses with tambours and siding, I could never be an architect? Do you think the orthopedist started out saying that his dream would never come true because he had never seen the Pitié-Salpêtrière hospital and that the only thing he knew about medicine was the medical centre in Saint-Pierre? You're feeling sorry for yourself, that's what you're doing." He paused for a short moment before delivering the final blow. "Really, you can do better than that."

He was angered by her lack of confidence. She could not bear the idea of disappointing him any further by letting him think she had no hopes for the future, so she murmured: "I do have an idea."

"There! I knew it. Tell me..."

"I want...Well, I'd like..."

"Come on, say it!"

He had never seen her at a loss for words.

She sat up straight in her uncomfortable chair, looked him straight in the eye and, no longer the need to whisper, announced loudly and clearly: "I want to be a writer."

"Well then, what are you waiting for? Do it."

He did not even seem surprised. As if it were that simple! As if she had said: "I want to be a teacher."

"You're not shocked?"

"Why would that shock me? If it's what you want to do, and I don't doubt it for a second, I say go ahead. Do it! The most important thing is knowing what you want."

"Do it." She had never believed those two words could have such a powerful effect. She was expecting something completely different, along the lines of: "It's a nice idea, but don't you think you're being unreasonable?" Or perhaps, "Maybe later, but first you need to get a job." The same trite phrases that her parents would say, she was sure of that.

"Do it." It was as simple as that. No ifs or buts. Two words that gave her wings. But on the other hand, they meant there was no escape.

While all this was bouncing around in her head like a ball on the Zakpiat Bat, where men on the island played the game of Basque pelota, François looked at her calmly. It was as though he was watching doors open wide in front of her eyes. He saw in her eyes the light-ning-fast rising of hope.

Knowing that he had to give it time to work itself out, he pushed back his chair and stood up, inviting her to do the same.

"Let's go. The doctor is waiting for us."

"Twenty-three thousand photos, exactly," announced the curator. "Twenty-five years of work."

"And there is not a single person in any of them," she whispered in François' ear. She looked at the crosses, statues, calvaries—all silhouettes against the leaden skies.

Doctor Louis Thomas, who had followed the Terre-Neuvas across the sea, the soldiers out to the front, the freedom fighters in Spain, and the prisoners in concentration camps, had spent the last part of his career on a lifeless art in which Man was present only in the frozen expression of his pain and his naive hope for a better world.

"Perhaps he had lost his faith in humanity..." said François.

"Surely that is true, to some extent. But not completely. He chose to show that men dream of the world beyond, of what is most beautiful, most pure. He could have chosen to take pictures of nature..."

"Really, though!" cried François, exasperated. "Here is a man who took part in all the struggles, whose thirst for learning is insatiable, who fights *La Morue française* to defend the poor beachboys, sails for months around the banks, puts war on trial in his photos, never shies away from taking a risk...and here this man ends his life like this, in a kind of solitary contemplation. You can't say it's not strange."

"It certainly is," agreed Émilie, pensive.

Sitting in the curator's office, surrounded by cases upon cases of prints, negatives, and films, they were trying to outline the shape of this impressive collection.

"Look at this angle, this atmosphere," he exclaimed with admiration. "What talent!"

"Calvary in the Fouesnant forest, 1956," she read. "During his last years, near the end of the collection."

When they returned to François' office, an urgent message from his researcher was waiting for him. François hurried to call her back.

"I just found some information about the doctor. He died in a hospital in Saint-Nazaire two years ago. He has an adopted daughter. I just contacted her."

"An adopted daughter?" he cried, looking at Émilie with astonishment. "And you talked to her?"

"Yes, and she offered to bring us some material Doctor Thomas left her."

"What kind of material?"

"Glass plates of Saint-Pierre et Miquelon, she told me, and some personal papers."

"Did you make arrangements to meet her?"

"Yes, tomorrow. She lives in a suburb of Paris and she seemed thrilled that someone was interested in her father. She couldn't wait to talk to us. She said he had suffered a lot from the fact that there wasn't much interest in his work."

François hung up the phone.

"The mystery is unravelling," he announced. He was clearly relieved. He took her hand to tell her the latest news.

The next morning, a woman in her sixties arrived at the office. She was very tall, very elegant, with beautiful grey hair carefully pulled back into a tidy bun, and her face was so gentle that it seemed to invite strangers to confide in her.

Émilie could read all this in the instant it took the visitor to introduce herself, make herself comfortable in an armchair, and place an old leather bag at her feet.

"It's his briefcase," she confirmed, following Émilie's gaze. He had it the day we arrived in Le Havre—him, mama, and I in 1926. In it, you'll see, there is a series of glass plates, a few albums, and some papers.

"Excuse me," said Émilie, taken aback. "But you said you disembarked in Le Havre with him. So..." she was a little embarrassed to ask. "So his wife and his daughter didn't travel with him?"

"Oh yes, they were there. I can remember it as if it were yesterday. Marthe, their daughter, was my age, thirteen. Mama and the doctor met during the crossing, and when they arrived on the wharf, he left his wife and daughter to come with us."

"That's incredible!"

"Yes," she admitted, with a sad little smile. She turned to François. "My mother and I were coming back from a trip to Canada. My father was Canadian. He and my mother separated soon after I was born and she had taken me to meet him. In the months before the trip,

I could feel my mother becoming very depressed. And then, after a few days on the ship, everything changed. From one day to the next, she had completely changed. When we got to Le Havre I figured out why."

"And the doctor?"

"I met him for the first time the day we arrived. In the morning, when we were packing up, my mother told me that she had met someone who made her happy. Then she introduced me to the doctor. He was quite embarrassed. I think he was worried about how I was going to react. And the whole thing had probably made him quite upset."

"I'm not surprised!" François burst out without thinking.

"Yes, I know," she sighed. "But for my mother and me, all we had was each other, for so long. I adored her and she had been so unhappy that when I saw her so light-hearted, so energetic, so excited, I was relieved. The doctor had such a good face; I could tell he wouldn't do anything to hurt us, and that we would be happy together."

"What about his family?"

"Oh, it was terrible. On the wharf, my mother and I were on one side, his wife and his daughter on the other. Even though she was upset, Mrs. Thomas stood straight and tall; she was very dignified. But Marthe's expression was unbearable. Put yourself in her place. The doctor tried to talk to her, to explain, her mother encouraged her to listen, but there was nothing anyone could do. 'From now on,' she told her father, 'you no longer exist.' Then she turned her back on him and walked away. The doctor let her go, but I saw him staggering. And my mother, as discreetly as possible, took him by the hand. Mrs. Thomas and her daughter climbed into a car and the three of us watched them leave. The doctor squeezed my mother's hand so hard his knuckles were white. I took my mother's arm and together we formed a wall against his pain."

"And after that?"

"We went our own way. From that moment on, we were a family. We were so close, so happy together. I only understood later, during the last few years of his life, that the doctor's new life had saved him from despair."

"Did he ever see his first family again?"

"He saw Mrs. Thomas, who had become a doctor herself, during the war. She had taken refuge in Algeria, and he had spent long periods of time there when he was in the Resistance. Marthe always refused to see him. When he was dying, I contacted her, hoping she would be able to forgive him, but she refused to come, just as she refused her inheritance. She had had such a sad life, lived alone, never wanted to start a family."

"The doctor must have been so hurt by that."

"Yes, it was a wound that never healed. His daughter's pain was a burden on him, although in the last part of his life he was more serene. He talked to me about her in the last few days of his life."

"What happened to your mother?"

"She died several years before he did. He took care of her, all by himself, with an extraordinary devotion. They meant everything to each other. After Le Havre, they were never apart, not for a single moment. They were both passionate about photography, and they went all over Brittany together, making an inventory of religious monuments throughout the region. That was the doctor's last project. When mama knew she was dying, she was really worried about what would happen to him. She was afraid he wouldn't want to go on without her. At the time, her reaction seemed excessive to me, but I realized afterwards how close he had come to ending his life on the ship in 1926. That's when I understood the role my mother had played at that time."

"Does the fact that we're doing research on him upset you?" asked Émilie, who was a little ashamed to be bringing such intimate details of the doctor's story to light.

"Not at all! The doctor deserves to be better understood. He never tried to explain the decision he made on the wharf in Le Havre, why he made such a dramatic change in his life. In a way, he never really forgave himself. That's why he never tried to get back in touch with his friends in Saint-Pierre et Miquelon. He talked about them all the time, though. I never went there, but I know all about the places he loved: Langlade, Mirande, Miquelon, le Chapeau, le Barachois...It's as though he had gone into exile," she added with the conviction of someone who sees injustice and suffers from it. "And besides, he deserved to have people take an interest in him and his work while he was still alive. Nobody did. If you want to honour him today, that is a good thing. The only person who might keep me from giving you this material is Marthe, and she has made it perfectly clear that she is no longer part of the family."

"Would you like to stay here while we look at them, at least?" asked François.

"No, thank you. I already know every detail by heart. I'd rather let you look at them yourselves. You know where to find me, and I can come back if you need me."

She stood up. As she turned to say goodbye, her eyes were drawn to one of the photos hanging on the wall, the one of the doctor sitting on the capstan with the seal in his arms. She went up to look at it.

"It would be good if people in Saint-Pierre et Miquelon knew what happened to him. He loved them so."

She went out, her eyes filled with tears. Émilie realized that this woman must be the spitting image of her mother at the same age. She and François sat down together, the briefcase in front of them, rather intimidated by the idea that it might contain answers to their questions, and also the end of the road.

"Jacques should be with us now," she murmured.

"We'll show him when he gets here," replied François.

He pulled the worn briefcase, its leather soft with age, delicately towards him. He unfastened the two straps, then took out the albums and handed Émilie the letters.

There was really not much there. A few official letters from the department of the Navy, some notes to accompany various glass plates, letters from Emma that gave news of Marthe, and a little package of envelopes tied up in a ribbon that Émilie undid with the greatest care possible.

"What's in it?" asked François, intrigued.

"They're letters addressed to people in Saint-Pierre et Miquelon," she replied, leafing through them. "One for Auguste Maufroy, another for Paul Chartier, one for Dominique Borotra, and one for Ernest Hutton. They're all stamped and ready to be mailed..."

"And he never mailed them..."

Delicately, she opened one of the envelopes and took out the letter addressed to Auguste Maufroy.

Dear Auguste...

Except for the greeting, the page was blank. She quickly opened the other envelopes. It was the same thing: *Dear Paul, Dear Dominique...*and then nothing.

"He didn't write anything!" she cried. "He addressed the envelopes, wrote the greetings, and that's it!"

"He didn't know what to say."

François had long since stopped looking at the albums, which contained photos that he had not seen before but which were not much different from thousands of others the doctor had abandoned on the islands. Émilie held the envelopes on her lap, vain attempts to reconnect with the past.

François got up and turned some lights on while Émilie went to get a glass of water, as if they absolutely had to move around to bring back some sense of reality, of the ordinary world, in order to soften the intensity of the moment. They sat down on the sofa next to each other. She leaned her head on his shoulder, hoping to be comforted a bit from the pain of this man who had never found the words to reconnect with his islands. In the rust-coloured light of the lamp, in the silence of the building that the employees had left hours ago, a feeling of serenity descended on them.

"He must have suffered so deeply from not being able to reconnect with the people he cared about," she sighed.

He stroked her shoulder without saying anything.

"At least we have a chance to honour him now. Everyone will be able to admire his life and his work, and realize what an exceptional man he was."

"And they'll finally know what happened to him," she said.

"We owe it to him..."

And François, who had never been a fan of words any more than of confidences, added: "He made me aware of a lot of things," he said, casting his gaze on the luxury of his office. "For a long time I thought financial and social success was all I needed. If we hadn't met the doctor, I would no doubt have kept on working like a mule. Fortunately, this adventure has taught me something, a new way of enjoying life, appreciating the beauty of friendship...and of you."

She smiled and gave him a look that was so full of tenderness that he felt that he was powerful enough to change his life for the better. For him, now over fifty years old, the world was opening up new and unexpected possibilities, as exciting as the day when, as a young scholarship student, he stood on the deck of the ship that was taking him to France, watching the islands disappear behind him as his future spread out before him on the horizon.

"I've made a decision...One I've been thinking of since you got here. And here it goes: I've done enough here. I'm going to pass the business over to one of my associates and I'm going to do something else."

"What?" she asked, her eyes wide with astonishment.

"I don't know yet, but I can tell you that I'm going to be spending more time in Saint-Pierre. I'd like to do something in heritage preservation there, or maybe teach. Why not? A completely different way of life, anyway, as I see it. I know what I don't want to do. Life is too short, and I don't want to have regrets all my life the way the doctor did." He suddenly sat up straight and asked, in an excited voice, "Do you think that Edmond would like me to design a museum for him?"

She smiled knowingly. "You know he's not the type

to refuse an offer like that!"

"Well, I'll start there," he said, thrilled with his idea. "Then we'll see. And you?"

"Me, too. If it weren't for the doctor and you, I would have missed out on what's essential," she whispered like a confession.

"And the essential, for you, would be...?"

"To get over my fears, to come here and study, to see if I can measure up to others...to succeed."

For a brief moment, it seemed as if, on top of his capstan, a small smile appeared on Doctor Thomas' face.

Six months later, François arrived at his mother's house for lunch. He had spent the morning in the land registry and the public works offices in Saint-Pierre, examining the piece of land where the new museum would soon be built. As was to be expected, Edmond had enthusiastically agreed to François' offer to design a museum. "And he's a local son, too!" he had exclaimed. They were still looking for funding, but neither Edmond nor François viewed that as a serious obstacle. The exhibition in France of Doctor Thomas' photographs had rallied political will for the construction of a new museum, and the purse-strings seemed to be loosening up.

François began his project with great enthusiasm, feeling that his new life and the light-heartedness it brought him would strengthen his creativity, or even transform it completely. He was tremendously eager to get to the drawing board.

As he explained to Edmond, "It's almost as if it's my very first contract!"

As he entered his home that morning, he noticed

the mail had been put on the little table next to the telephone. There was a large envelope addressed to him. "Émilie!" he cried. Since she had moved to Paris in September, she kept him informed of everything she was discovering, and entertained him with silly stories about getting used to the big city and the university. She was staying in his apartment. "Why look for an apartment," he told Émilie's parents, "when mine is free? When I visit, it is plenty big for two people."

My, she's on a roll! he thought, looking at the size of the envelope. He opened it impatiently. There was a Clairefontaine notebook in it, one of those school notebooks with a margin and lines to keep the notes clear and organized.

On the first page, in the still uncertain handwriting of a teenage girl, were a few words carefully underlined with such a straight line it was obvious that it had been made with a ruler. It read: *The Islands of Doctor Thomas.* He hurried to turn the page. On it was a photo, the one of Cap Blanc in the winter, followed by a handwritten text. Further on he found the photo of the doctor on the capstan with the seal on his lap; further still a pebble beach in Miquelon, near the church. And at the end, the incredible portrait of the doctor. A written passage accompanied each photo.

Miquelon
February 10, 1913

I took off from the village as though the Devil were at my heels. I took refuge here, on top of a little hillock, where I am looking at the nature around me, frozen into ice. My camera is at my feet. Glacial, immobile, nature seems to be crying out to me: "Why did you come here?"

In the Doctor's House, *as people in Miquelon call it with deep respect in their voice, Emma is resting, our little Marthe snuggled in her arms. She was born last night. Emma, who was calm and serene throughout her pregnancy, gave birth the same way, without screaming or fighting, a very simple birth. "It's not an illness," she likes to say. "Childbirth is not necessarily painful." She certainly proved it to me. I was feverishly awaiting this birth, filled with joy to bring into the world the flesh of my flesh. It's a privilege that most men don't have a chance to experience the way I did.*

The whole world was peaceful around us. The old midwife from Miquelon was even discreet enough to leave me alone with my wife once she had checked to see that the baby was presenting normally. The miracle of the birth of our first child took place in the privacy of our own bedroom, the same place where she had been conceived.

When I saw the head of the baby emerge from its cocoon, with a beautiful full head of hair, I took the tiny shoulders in my hand and I turned the tiny, slippery body around. I was thunderstruck by a happiness which must be akin to God's when he created the Earth in his image. Our little girl slipped into my open hands with a confidence that was all the proof I needed that we would be united in infinite love.

The moment I raised my head to reassure Emma and to tell her that we had a baby girl, I felt as though I was the master of the world. I was certain that my heart would never be big enough to contain all the love I had for these two women.

An instant later, after I held our daughter by the feet and gave her a little tap in the back, all this happiness brutally and inexplicably transformed into an intolerable pain. I looked at the little face, contorted with pain, the anguished cries of this child who had been taken away from the reassuring sound of her mother's heartbeat, who was forced to learn how to breathe on her own, thrown into the world, and I was conscious of the enormity of what Emma and I had done. What right did we have to bring this child into the world? What sorrows would she have to endure? And at the very moment I was asking myself these disturbing questions, trying to appease my

*fears and relieve my remorse, I put my face close to hers. I
felt instinctively that this wrinkled face was like the one
my daughter would have at the time of her death. I
wanted to howl with fear. When her blind eyes stared
back at me, I wanted to die.*

*How can the horror of this vision be explained? How can
it be explained, especially to the woman who is, at that
very moment, exhausted by the delivery and flooded with
a new and overwhelming motherly love for her child, who
has closed her eyes and rests, smiling and comfortable on
her pillow? What could be said to the midwife who, seeing
me rush out of the room, attributed my emotion to pride
and a desire to tell everyone we had a little girl?*

*I kept the horror of my thoughts to myself. I would have
been ashamed to share them. During the hours that .
followed—it seemed like centuries—I shook hands and
accepted congratulations, embraced Emma and kissed the
forehead of the little victim that I had forced to live and
that I barely dared to look at for fear of having a vision
of the apocalypse.*

*That is how I came to be here, on top of this hill. Emma
looked at me with a tired smile as I left. Because she is
always pragmatic, I don't doubt for an instant that she
believes my instability is due to a combination of fatigue
and exaltation. The people of Miquelon would probably
see it as more proof of my being odd: "He doesn't do
anything the same way as the rest of us," they will say,
shaking their heads.*

*I am crying. I am thinking about my patients who struggle
day after day for their bread, sitting in a dory clutching
their fishing line, who, at the end of their day on the sea,*

lean over a pebbly plot of land to pull up carrots, potatoes, or cabbage, who hunt, gather, build, repair, knit, sew, and cook to survive. They couldn't care less about my state of mind. I feel guilty.

At the end of a long while, drowning in tears, I raise my eyes to the horizon. I observe that on this day after another storm, even nature cannot take any more. Not a wave on the exhausted ocean, not a ray of the weak sun, too tired to make the slightest effort, and no warmth in these freezing hills on which, you would swear, no bakeapple will ever ripen again, these icy ponds on which no ducks or geese will ever again land, or this brush in which no deer or rabbit will ever again hide.

Several minutes pass. Little by little, however, in the calm of nature, I can feel serenity emerge from below the frozen surface. Quietly, patiently, in the ineffable beauty of my surroundings, in spite of the heavy cloud cover and the biting cold, I begin to feel comforted. Beauty and suffering are one, each existing only because of the other. Nature is beautiful because it is sad. The cold that invades each of my pores makes me dream of the warmth of the house I have just fled.

Over there in the distance, despite the ocean that is pretending to be docile, the lighthouse at Cap Blanc keeps watch over the sailors. It keeps watch over the fishers, just as I will keep watch over Marthe. Why did I run away? Why was I so frightened?

I am getting the photo ready. Through my camera, will I be able to express what I have just understood: That without horror, there is no beauty; without fear, no true love; without danger, no real attachment? The horror of *our condition is exactly this—in order to appreciate one, we must inflict the other upon ourselves.*

One day, I will try to explain all this to Marthe. Perhaps, then, she will forgive us...

Miquelon
March 1915

I let him do it. I shouldn't have let him.

*"Take it, Doctor, take it! Your lady will take a photo of
you," he said as he put the young seal he had just caught
in the barachois, no doubt after killing its mother, into my
arms. "One less," he probably said, as he took back the
bloody carcass. Seals are the fisherman's enemy. I've never
really understood why. He will take the skin, which he'll
put in his dory, "to keep us warm in the bad weather,
there's nothing better." The meat will feed the dogs. As for
the baby seal, "it will entertain the children," he must
have thought as he ran across the sand bank to catch it.*

*And here I am, sitting on the capstan with the little
creature in my arms. I can feel the desperate beating of its
heart. The terror. Its and my own.*

"Smile," says Emma. I can't. Marthe is sitting right beside

*her and is dying to hold the little animal in her arms. She
is not allowed. "They bite hard," a fisherman explained.
"Smile, Louis," insisted Emma. I know I can't, but I am
trying to anyway. And when I am almost succeeding, the
little seal cries and its lament grabs me.*

*Suddenly I can hear the terrified screams of the men lying
in agony at the bottom of the trenches, these strong and
courageous men who had been sent to the front to kill the
enemy and who, as they lay dying, called out for their
mothers: "Mama." The efforts the seal is making to get out
of my arms awakes in me the memory of these bodies that
shudder just before they die, their moans, their laments
that they can barely get out of their throat that
was constricted with the agony of dying, the geysers of
blood that spurted up and half-drowned their howls. All
of this comes back to me, carrying me off like a strong
undercurrent, while the people before me make kind
attempts to make me smile. "The poor man is never happy
for long. He's been like this since he got back from the war."*

*A long cry stirs in the very depths of my bowels. I want to
jump down to the ground, throw myself in the water with
this little animal, save the life of this innocent creature; so
often I have to be satisfied with being there for them when
injured men are dying and I can't do anything else for
them.*

*Like all the other public employees of France who are
posted to Saint-Pierre et Miquelon, I left as soon as war
was declared in 1914. The men of the islands were able to
stay home for a while yet, because they were exempted
from regular military service, but it wasn't long before they
joined us.*

As soon as I arrived in France, I was sent to the front with my scalpel and my camera. "What more could you ask for?" one of the army officers asked me. I was put in charge of treating the injured soldiers and recording images of the German defeats. "It won't take long," the officer concluded.

Is it fortunate that in the trenches we lose all sense of time? That the more time passes, the less important it seems to measure it? After all, what is important is to survive, when more and more death surrounds us. The best we can hope for is to die quickly and with dignity, if possible. But in the mud and the darkness, under hails of bullets and bombs and on the ground shaken by shells, it seemed to me that there was no dignity possible. I saw hundreds of men die in misery, not understanding what was happening to them or why they were fighting. "Died for France." There was always some man in uniform to utter these words while his companions in arms would be silent for a moment, praying for his soul and thanking the heavens that they had escaped death for one more moment. In my case, I would bow my head and ask, Why? I never found the answer.

A few months ago I was slightly injured and sent here, to Miquelon, to recover in this calm little place which had experienced war only through the heartbreaking telegrams announcing the death of a brother, a father, a friend who "perished in the line of duty." Here there were no shells, no retreats from the enemy or howls of anguish, no men fainting or soiling themselves at the horrific sight of the battleground, no limbs scattered along the bottoms of trenches, no clenched fists surfacing above a body buried in the mud, the wedding band still gleaming. In

Miquelon, war is an abstract concept. Certainly life is hard and the ocean is often cruel. In my arms, this little creature which is afraid it's going to die cries like a baby.

"Smile!" Emma urges gently. I try. Trying is all I can do. I try to fit back into the normal course of life, pretending it has not changed forever; I try to get interested in life again after seeing all this horror. A horror I am unable to share. It would be unthinkable for me to impose on those I loved the drama they had not experienced. I do not know how to explain my devastation, my despair to Emma. She has watched my physical wounds heal and believes, wrongly, that I am better.

Like the other men who have returned from battle, I do nothing to explain. I cannot talk about it. We all live behind a wall of silence. Some throw themselves into work as soon as they get their strength back. Others, in an attempt to appease their frenzy, will throw themselves into the sea as soon as possible. The doctor that I am recognizes the symptoms but can do nothing. There is no cure for human cruelty.

The only treatment I know is to try to live, to smile, if only to avoid spreading the cancer any further. I try but today smiling is not possible. Before the war I was invaded by melancholy from time to time, but there was always a touch of beauty somewhere in my world: in nature or in the eyes of my daughter, a glimmer of light to chase away the darkness. Since I've been back, I've searched desperately for a bit of light, and have found none. Everything is sadness. Sometimes Emma hands me my camera and encourages me to go outside. For years, I could find beauty in the stark landscape of the islands, a ray of sun peeking from behind the clouds or sparkling on fresh fallen snow, the dignity of a man of the sea, the courage of a fisherman's wife. Everywhere, always, I wanted to see and show the beauty hidden under the ugliness. Today, I am no longer looking for it. In the bottom of the trenches, I ended my quest, overcome by the horrors of war.

My camera no longer holds any interest for me. My friend Dominique, who was so pleased when I introduced him to photography, feels abandoned. Together we walked all over Miquelon and photographed every nook and cranny, then retreated to the little darkroom set up in his attic. There, in the dim space lit only by a tiny window covered by a piece of red fabric, we spent hours together watching the splendours of the islands and its courageous inhabitants emerge in the prints. Today, I can rarely go outside, and I hardly ever take photos. Most of all, I refuse to shut myself off in the attic. My former refuge has become a prison. I cannot stand closed doors or, even worse, the darkness.

In my arms, the little seal is no longer wrestling with me. It has figured out that it will not escape. It is resigned to its fate. So am I. Emma takes the photo. I can tell she is exasperated. She knows that smiling is beyond me today. "The doctor is so sad ever since he came home from the war," the fisherman will say to his wife tonight over a bowl of soup. "But I think that I cheered him up a little by giving him the little seal to hold. I wanted to take it back after the photo was taken, but he didn't let me. He said he was going to look after him."

The Beachboys

His name was Ange-Marie and it suited him. When they called me to his bedside, it was already too late. The head of the beachboys had waited before calling me. He was sure that Ange-Marie was pretending. That's what he told me, without a shadow of regret, no doubt believing that I would simply accept his explanation. As though it was natural to think a thirteen-year-old boy who had worked non-stop for two months was lazy, normal to suspect he was faking it when he was writhing in pain on the pile of disgusting straw that was his only bed! I lit into this cruel man, who in reply walked out of the cabin, still muttering under his breath that he had better things to do than listen to me.

Since I arrived in Saint-Pierre et Miquelon, how many men have I seen like this, whose abscesses, coughs, fevers I'm supposed to cure so they can get back to the hard labour of their work on the shore? They ask me, a medical doctor, to attack the symptoms without ever treating the causes.

The colleagues I have now and those who preceded us—with the possible exception of the most blind or vile—as well as the physicians who work on the naval ships or for the Seamen charities have made the same observation for years: the living conditions of the Terre-Neuvas and the beachboys are horrific and are the main causes of the serious illnesses we find on the banks and on the islands.

The ship owners from Saint-Malo and Granville and the big businessmen from the islands are responsible for the deplorable hygiene in the shacks that beachboys are crammed into. In their eyes, these men, despite being workmen who make them rich, do not deserve much consideration. Especially since for every beachboy that dies there are dozens of others waiting to take his place. So why change anything?

I arrived too late to save Ange-Marie, whom I didn't know. There are so many of them and they all look the same, with their ragged, filthy clothes and the glassy, alcoholic look in their eyes. It's hard to tell them apart. The straggly herd reminds me of the contingents of new recruits that arrived every few weeks at the front. This poor boy died holding my hand, terrified by the approaching death, his eyes glued to mine in mute interrogation. Here in Miquelon, as in the trenches, I had no answers.

Walking back up from the shore, on my way to fill out the death certificate, I took a deep breath of spring air, in the ever-present odour of salt cod, this cod in front of which everyone bows down and salutes, this cod that kills.

I watched as a flock of superb gannets rose over the

roadstead. They were circling and spinning around the blue spring sky like kites carried by the wind, indifferent to the horrors of the unending war in France and to the misery of the poor boys and men who, in a dilapidated cabin, gathered around the mutilated body of this child who looked like a battered old man. Had these wild birds flying free come to take the body of the angelic child into the heavens? In any case, I saw it as one more sign of encouragement.

Since gazing into the eyes of that dying child, I know what I have to do. On the next mail ship to France, I will send a letter to my superiors at the department responsible for the Navy, with the report I have been preparing for a while about the situation of the beachboys. I only regret not being able to include some of the photos I have taken to illustrate my statements. Out of respect for the profession and for the dignity of my patients, I never took my camera into their shacks. And yet, I am sure that these images would speak much louder than all the pages of my report.

For years, all the doctors who have been posted to Saint-Pierre have called for improvements to be made to the housing, the working conditions, the food, and the treatment of these young boys at the hands of their bosses. And then the doctors leave, without seeing any change at all to the situation. I will not wait any longer!

After experiencing the horrors of the battleground, which still haunt me, I will no longer tolerate the cruelty of men for any reason, and especially not for more profit. Ange-Marie Ollivier will not have died in vain. It pains Emma to see the misery around us, lavishing attention and affection on Marthe as if to transfer a little bit of the love she feels for all these poor souls to her own child. I know she will support me in what I am doing.

I no longer accept the idea of horror and cruelty being everywhere in the world, especially if I can do something about it. This morning, anger and the desire to act have shaken me out of the lethargy to which I had resigned myself. Yes, there are things I can do. I must struggle at all costs against the despair that fills me a little more each day.

Leaving

The photographer wants me to smile. His request brings back a memory from fifteen years earlier. In 1915, in Miquelon, when Emma told me the same thing.

I have been back in France for four years now, but I am still carrying within me the pain of exile, a constant homesickness for Saint-Pierre et Miquelon. I dream of the islands where I am no longer living, where I spent only six years and five months of my existence. How is it possible to feel exiled when you are in your homeland? What can I do about it, since I have no way of reconnecting with that life?

When I left Saint-Pierre, on May 17, 1926, I had no regrets. The islands were living through the Prohibition. The islands whose inhabitants had built a life from the sea had fallen into the pitfalls of gin, rum, and whisky. I no longer felt like I belonged there. There was plenty of work—illnesses had changed, but not the patients—but I barely recognized my islands from before the war.

Prohibition had at least changed one thing for the best. Since alcohol had replaced fish, La Morue française *had lost its hold on the population. It is for this reason that I had been able to come back so easily in 1923, I'm sure.*

In these islands that I no longer recognized, my melancholy grew instead of disappearing. I couldn't figure out how to shake off my sadness. Day after day, Emma waited impatiently for the man I had been before to return to her side, and Marthe hunted for her father behind my devastated eyes. I could see it in their worried expressions, the care they took not to talk too loud, not to annoy me, the way you look after a patient who must be spared any emotion or inconvenience. Their precautions exasperated me, but I couldn't do anything to improve my state of mind. I was trapped in a heavy fog and couldn't find my way out. In a leap of courage, I had started taking photos again, but all I managed to capture was this omnipresent sadness. Maybe if I could have left Saint-Pierre and gone back to my post in Miquelon, things would be better. But another doctor had replaced me there.

Our three-year post was about to come to an end. I had rather brusquely told my superiors I did not want my post to be renewed. They were surprised, to say the least. In the wake of my outburst about La Morue française *in 1916, I had had to fight tooth and nail to get them to agree to send me back to Saint-Pierre et Miquelon. My superiors believed that I would never want to leave. However, they accepted my decision and repatriated us to France. We packed our bags in the spring. Wasn't a change of scenery supposed to be the best cure for all kinds of ailments?*

I put hundreds of photographic plates into storage. Because we didn't know yet where we would be living in Europe, Auguste Maufroy agreed to store them for me until I had a permanent address. I kept about a hundred photos of the islands, of fishing, of smuggling with me, thinking vaguely about publishing a book that I could write in my spare time. But I didn't really believe it. Today, I realize that selecting photos would be a way of avoiding a true separation with the islands. At the time, I must have had a sense that I would never be back.

Our little family was living under a shadow. Emma and I barely spoke, other than to mutter a few banal words about daily life. After struggling for months to bring me back to life, my companion had given up. Who could blame her? Had she figured out that, even more than war, it was life itself that horrified me? In any case, she had thrown in the towel and left me to my nostalgic apathy. I would have liked to do something about it, if only to put a smile on Marthe's face. At thirteen, she looked worried beyond her years. But I was incapable of doing anything about it.

We embarked on a sad, grey day that matched our moods perfectly. Standing on the deck, watching Le Colombier *disappear over the horizon, I turned a page of my life. There was no going back.*

In New York, we got on the passenger ship that would carry us back to Le Havre. Marthe and Emma, marvelling at the luxury of the ship and the many distractions it offered, left me alone with my thoughts. I was relieved, both for them and for me. I preferred to be alone.

I spent long hours standing by the railing, contemplating the foam on the nose of the ship, the eternal image of the ephemeral. The sea, which had accompanied me every day

*of my life—from my precious childhood souvenirs of
Landerneau, of sailing on dories, of medical visits to the
Grand Banks. The ocean, my great comforter. During the
crossing, I often considered jumping into it, like a playful
child jumps into his mother's arms, to let myself be rocked
or lulled by its waves, driven ahead by the powerful
propellers I could feel beneath the ship. I felt so alone. Even
Marthe, my dear Marthe, could do nothing for me.*

*One particular black night, I went to the very back of the
ship on the deck right above the propellers. Far behind us,
you could see the wake of the ship, a straight line that
formed a hyphen between this world and the world beyond.
I had decided to end it all. I could no longer battle the
suffocating feeling that strangled me every moment.
Suddenly, behind me, I heard the rustle of a skirt, followed
by a loud voice telling me: "It would be such a shame!"*

*I turned around as though I were a naughty child caught
misbehaving. A woman was looking straight at me. Her
sad expression showed that she had guessed my intentions,
although I had done nothing to suggest what I was about
to do. I hadn't even moved. I had only decided to do it.*

*She could have talked, in an attempt to diffuse my
melancholy. Instead, she simply smiled and reached out her
hand, which I took without a moment's hesitation, like a
drowning man grabbing onto a buoy. As I felt her hand,
the lump of despair that cut me off from the world burst
open. In the dark night that enveloped us, I felt, for the
first time in a long time, flooded with light. I smiled. I was
no longer alone. A door had opened.*

*How difficult it is to explain what happened to us both, in
that instant, unless it is to say with certainty that our lives*

had changed, that we had each found an anchor, and that no one and nothing could take us back to the past.

That evening, we were two days away from Le Havre. For nearly forty-eight hours I thought about the future, looking in Emma's and Marthe's eyes for a link that would still join me to them, waiting for the moment that my reason would take control again, when I would see that my emotion was simply a product of my fatigue and I would go back onto the road laid out before me. In vain. I felt that I was linked to this woman that I didn't even know but with whom, finally, everything seemed possible again.

On the grey wharf of Le Havre, I set down the little suitcase that contained my books and the precious glass plates. Then I helped Emma, ever stoic, and Marthe, who was crushed, to gather their belongings and set off to the train station. I should have felt ashamed, hesitated and cried out to them to come back. Instead, as I watched them leave, I felt such relief and peace that it was as if I had wings. After ten years of darkness, life was starting over.

Four years have gone by since then. When I look into the lens or at a photographer who is asking me to smile, I know that I have no regrets. I am alive. Without this unexpected encounter, I know that this wouldn't be the case. But in order to open the door to my future I had to close another one on the past, and I know in doing so I caused unforgiveable pain to those I loved.

Emma and Marthe live at the other end of France. Emma studied medicine and opened a medical office in a little country village. Marthe is attending a school hardly bigger than the one in Miquelon. Wheat fields have replaced hills, and ponds the beaches on the west shore and those of the

Grand Barachois. She has a black cat like the one she had in Saint-Pierre, the one she had in the picture I took of her in the snow. Emma writes to me from time to time, telling me about their daily life. That's it. She doesn't hold any grudges. She knew, long before we got to Le Havre, that I had slipped away from her. My daughter, however, can't forgive me and refuses to see me. To protect her, we won't divorce. Because of this, there will be no place for me and my companion in high society in France.

This is the price of happiness: absence, exile, the inability to build a proper life in France where, in any case, I do not feel at home. My companion lived across the Atlantic as well for many years and shares my discomfort. Our place is in France, even though we find it too limited. My career, her daughter and mine are all here. Our shared happiness justifies the sacrifice.

I would have had to write to get back some of the glass plates I left in Saint-Pierre. I would have to write to Auguste Maufroy. I can't imagine how uncomfortable it would feel to think of this envelope being placed in the mail bag, sent across the ocean to the islands, and arriving on his desk. My name would be whispered throughout the town: "Heavens! A letter from Doctor Thomas!" That doctor no longer exists. My friends from that life would no doubt have little respect for the one I have become.

In any case, the photos would simply remind me of unbearable memories of another life: Marthe playing with her little cat in the snow, Emma horseback riding in the Goulet, a photo taken with Dominique, the beachboys in Folquet, the salt works of Pointe au Cheval, snow-covered Cap Blanc, coming back from hunting in Miquelon...

Leaving (end)

I have turned the corner of my eightieth year. I am a tired traveller on the platform of a train station. My body is not suffering but my tortured mind is begging for mercy. I have taken refuge in Brittany, in the comfort of a retirement home that looks out on the sea, and I am reexamining my life. Even if I would like to forget the mistakes I have made, I can't. Every day, at my side, a loving and caring woman sits by my side. Her gentle features remind me of the woman who saved me from my misery and, since then, has left me.

It has been more than ten years since she "closed her eyes," as they say in Saint-Pierre et Miquelon. I have never considered the possibility of following her, because she gave me the will to live. And then there was her daughter, towards whom I feel a father's responsibility. Now that illness has come, she is the daughter who sits with her adoptive father and brings him some relief in these

*difficult times. Her presence in my life is a great comfort.
At the same time, it cuts me to the quick. She and my own
daughter, Marthe, are the same age. I know nothing
about the flesh of my flesh. Since Emma's death, I have
had no news about her. I'm told she lives in the United
States, where she has taken a job as a teacher at a school
for young girls. She is not married, has no children, no
family at all now. She must lead a sad existence, and I am
to blame for that.*

*This evening, as night fell and drew us to confide in each
other, my adopted daughter and I talked about the ghosts
who inhabit my memory. This is how I learned that my
two daughters—I hope I can be forgiven for calling them
that—had met, a decade or so ago, on a transatlantic
ocean liner. One was coming home to France for the
holidays, the other had gone to visit her biological father.
Through one of those unexpected coincidences, they met on
the deck of the ship. They had not seen each other since
the fateful voyage of 1926, yet they recognized each other
instantly. One approached the other with the natural
confidence that happiness bestows on people. Marthe,
however, turned away and fled.*

*This confidence extinguished any hope I had of seeing
Marthe before I died. Curiously, accepting the fact calmed
me. I had no expectations now. My daughter could not
forgive my greatest sin, that of destroying her life so that I
could go and live mine, betraying her love in order to
follow mine. The day she was born, I had the unbearable
feeling that she would suffer, and the lightning-bright
intuition that I would be to blame.*

For many years, I tried to absolve myself. I put myself in

*harm's way with the Spanish republicans, I joined the
Resistance, I documented the horrors of human folly at the
gates of the concentration camps, all this in the hopes of
paying my debt. When, disgusted with the behaviour of
men, I tried to redeem them, and myself, by cataloguing
the artwork inspired by the divine, it seemed to me that
when I finished this task I would be absolved.*

*It was a useless battle. There is no absolution, and there is
no turning back. Every man's burden, as I understand it
this evening, is to move ahead, at any cost, and to carry
his sin for eternity. Even more, it is to know that he would
make the same error again, because the consequences of
not committing it would be even more serious and
painful. In the end, the unforgivable thing would have
been to not bother trying. I can go now. I hear the train. I
would like to return to Miquelon.*

Closing the notebook, tears in his eyes, François noticed
a letter sticking out of the envelope. He had missed it in
his rush to open the book and discover its treasures.

Dear François,

*You told me to "do it" last spring. I realized that the
doctor had also challenged me: "Tell them the story," he
seemed to say with that insistence in his eyes that you know
all too well. So, here, "I've done it!"*

Yours,
Émilie

He understood that she was beginning to soar.

Acknowledgements

Many individuals contributed to this novel. Thanks to Yves Leroy, who gave me many details on the life of Doctor Louis Thomas, and to Gracia Couturier, who early on helped me structure my ideas.

Thanks also to Muriel and Yvon in Miquelon and Harry in Prince Edward Island who gave me space and solitude to write. Finally, to all those, far and near, who helped me on this journey alongside Doctor Thomas, I owe my heartfelt gratitude.

Françoise Enguehard was born on the islands of Saint-Pierre et Miquelon. She is the author of the bestselling novel *Tales From Dog Island*, and has also published *Les petits plats dans les grands: l'art de la table a Saint-Pierre-et-Miquelon*, along with the young adult novels *Le tresor d'Elvis Bozec* and *Le pilot du Roy*.